John C. Lambert

Three Fishing Boats

and other talks to children

John C. Lambert

Three Fishing Boats
and other talks to children

ISBN/EAN: 9783337403669

Printed in Europe, USA, Canada, Australia, Japan

Cover: Foto ©Andreas Hilbeck / pixelio.de

More available books at **www.hansebooks.com**

THREE
FISHING BOATS

AND

Other Talks to Children

BY

Rev. JOHN C. LAMBERT, B.D.,

Author of "The Omnipotent Cross and other Sermons," &c.

New Edition.

Edinburgh and London:
OLIPHANT, ANDERSON, & FERRIER.

THE CHILDREN'S SUNDAY.

A New Series of Books for Young People.

Post 8vo, cloth extra. Price 1s. 6d. each.

Bible Stories without Names. By the Rev. HARRY SMITH. With Names on separate booklet at end.

The Children's Prayer. Addresses to the Young on the Lord's Prayer. By the Rev. JAMES WELLS, D.D.

Object Addresses for Church, Home, and School. By the Rev. A. HAMPDEN LEE.

Talks on Favourite Texts, and other Addresses to Children. By various Writers. Edited by the Rev. HARRY SMITH.

More Bible Stories without Names. By the Rev. HARRY SMITH.

THE "GOLDEN NAILS" SERIES.

Post 8vo, neat cloth. Price 1s. 6d. each.

Golden Nails, and other Addresses to Children. By the Rev. GEORGE MILLIGAN, B.D.

Pleasant Places: Words to the Young. By the Rev. R. S. DUFF, D.D.

Parables and Sketches. By ALFRED E. KNIGHT.

Silver Wings, and other Addresses to Children. By the Rev. ANDREW G. FLEMING.

Three Fishing Boats, and other Talks to Children. By the Rev. JOHN C. LAMBERT, B.D.

Lamps and Pitchers, and other Addresses to Children. By the Rev. GEORGE MILLIGAN, B.D.

A Bag with Holes, and other Addresses to Children. By the Rev. JAMES AITCHISON.

Kingless Folk, and other Addresses on Bible Animals. By the Rev. JOHN ADAMS, B.D.

The Little Lump of Clay, and other Five-Minute Talks to Children. By the Rev. H. W. SHREWSBURY.

The Oldest Trade in the World, and other Addresses to the Younger Folk. By the Rev. GEORGE H. MORRISON.

TO MY MOTHER.

PREFACE.

———◄◉►———

THE following addresses are such as the writer is in the habit of giving every Sabbath, at the morning service, to the children of his congregation. The circumstances of their production and delivery account for their brevity and want of elaboration. They are not intended as examples of what children's addresses ought to be; they are simply specimens of a kind of address which the writer has found helpful in increasing the interest of the children of his own congregation in the public worship of the church.

Perhaps it should be added, as an

explanation both of their matter and manner, that they were spoken mainly for the sake of the *younger* children. The writer, partly because of the unusual proportion of very young children in his morning audience, and partly because of his belief that older children are, in general, as appreciative of an ordinary sermon as their fathers and mothers, has found it most useful in the children's portion of the service to keep before his mind and heart those who are very young.

SUBJECTS.

Three Fishing Boats.

MANY of you when you were away for your summer holidays were staying at the seaside, and one of your chief pleasures there was to go out in a boat, especially if you had lines and bait so that you could "go a fishing." I daresay you have noticed, when two of you were fishing from opposite sides of the boat, that sometimes the fish came only to the one line, and left the other severely alone, until you began to think that the right side of the boat must be a better side to fish from than the left.

Last summer I was staying on the shores of Loch Fyne; and often, when I was out on the loch in the evenings, I saw a shoal of mackerel or herring passing quite near. Sometimes on the one side of the boat the water would be perfectly calm—not a fish to be seen; but on the other it seemed almost to be boiling with the jumping fish.

Well, one evening Peter and James and John and some other disciples went out in their boat to fish. They fished all night, but caught nothing. They hadn't even, it appears, a single fish for their own breakfast. Jesus came down to the shore, and He knew, although they did not, that there was a great shoal of fish on the right side of the boat. So He cried across the water, "Cast the net on the *right* side of the boat, and ye shall find." And now, when they cast the net, they could not draw it in, for the multitude of fishes.

Now, I want to speak to you for a few minutes about casting the net on the right side of the boat. I wish you to imagine that you are all fishermen. Sometimes the New Testament says that we are all to be soldiers, and again that we are all to be builders, and again that we are all to be travellers. But suppose at present that you are all fishers, and that Jesus comes to you and says when you are fishing, "Cast your net on the right side of the boat, and ye shall find."

Let me tell you of three boats in which boys and girls go out to fish.

1. The first I would call *the School-boat.*

As soon as you are old enough, you are put into this boat and launched out upon the wide sea; and your duty in this boat is to catch something. Can you tell me what it is? I think the name of it is *knowledge.* You would be very poor and helpless creatures by-and-by in this busy world, if you had no knowledge. And that is why your parents send you to school, and your teachers do their best to educate your minds.

But how are you to get this precious thing which is called knowledge? You must cast your net on the right side of the boat. For there is a right side and a wrong side in this school-boat. On the wrong side are the lazy children, and the idle children, and the inattentive children, and all the children who do not wish to learn. On the right side are the children who love knowledge, and do their best to gain it. And be sure of this, boys and girls, that if you cast your net on the right side of the boat, you are certain to find.

2. The second boat I call the *Business-boat.*

Some of the bigger boys have left

school now. We never see them going along the road, as they used to do, with large bundles of books. They have given up wearing their school caps, and have taken to felt hats; and they start by the train every morning along with the city men. And some of you, I know, have just finished your school-days, and are looking out at present for something to do. You are not sure what you are going to be, but at all events you are going into business.

Now can you tell me what people go to business for? "To make money," I think I hear you saying. But I say, "No! Not to make money merely, but to do *work*." Of course we must be paid for the work we do, or we could not live; but it is a very poor thing to work only for the money we get. We should work for the work's sake, because work is a noble thing in itself, and because every honest worker is serving God, and doing

B

good to his fellows, as well as benefiting himself.

Well, in this business-boat also there is a right side and a wrong side. The wrong side is the side of carelessness, and unpunctuality, and dishonesty. The right side is the very opposite of all these things. And if you cast your net on the right side of the boat, if you listen to the voice of Christ, and do what He tells you, you are certain to succeed. You may not make a great pile of money, and die a rich man; but God will send a blessing upon all your labour, and enable you to serve your own generation according to His will.

3. The third boat is *the Home-boat.*

This is the best boat of all. It is a boat for girls as well as for boys, for the old as well as for the young. And what can we catch in the home-boat? If the school-boat is for finding knowledge, and the business-boat for finding work, the home-boat, I think, is for finding *love*. God puts us into homes that we may learn to love, that parents may love their children, and children their parents, and brothers and sisters may love one another.

But in this beautiful home-boat there is a right side and a wrong side. The wrong side is the side of selfishness and disobedience, the right side is the side of obedience and love. Which side are you on, boys and girls? Remember that Jesus is watching you from the shore, and He is telling you what to do. If you will hearken to His voice, and cast your net on the right side of the boat, your homes will soon be full of a holy love which will make your lives both beautiful and bright.

The Hands of Jesus

————•◆•————

"Behold My hands."—LUKE xxiv. 39.

I WISH to speak to you this morning about the hands of Jesus. What wonderful hands they were! Wonderful for what they did, and wonderful for what they suffered. Will you listen for a little, while I tell you something about those blessed hands?

1. The hands of Jesus were *working hands*.

Jesus, as you know, is called the "Carpenter of Nazareth." There seems no doubt that for many long years before

He began His public ministry, He had been toiling patiently day by day in a carpenter's shop, and earning His bread by the labour of His hands. Most likely He began to work when He was quite a boy. Joseph and Mary were poor people ; they could not afford to keep Him long at school; and when He was no more than twelve years of age His school-days would all be over, and He would begin to learn His trade. Joseph at that time was the village carpenter. So Joseph took Jesus to be His own apprentice, and taught those boyish hands how to use the saw, and the hammer, and the chisel, and the plane. And by-and-by when Joseph died, it is very likely that Jesus, who was Mary's eldest son, became the chief support of His widowed mother and His orphan sisters. The burden of providing for a whole household rested now upon His young shoulders. And often, without doubt, He had to work

very long and very hard, until the sweat
poured down from His brow, and His
hands were sore and weary.

And thus Jesus becomes an example
to us of diligence in doing our everyday
work. Never be afraid or ashamed of
honest work. Only be afraid and ashamed
of laziness and carelessness in doing it.
Behold the hands of Jesus! Think of
that little workshop in Nazareth, and of
the great and holy Jesus toiling there so
patiently at the task which His Father
in heaven had given Him to do.

2. But again the hands of Jesus were
praying hands.

Paul says, in his First Epistle to
Timothy, that he would have men "pray
everywhere, lifting up holy hands." That
was exactly what Jesus did. His hands
were continually lifted up to God as
hands of prayer. When He left His
home in Nazareth, and went about the
country teaching, and preaching, and work-

ing miracles, He often was very busy—
so busy, we are told, that He had no
leisure even to eat bread. But He always
found time to pray. Sometimes, after
working hard all day long, He climbed
to the top of a high mountain, so as to
be alone with God, and spent the whole
night in earnest prayer.

And if the holy Jesus prayed so con-
stantly and fervently, how much need
we have to pray. I hope you boys and
girls do not forget to lift up to God the
hands of prayer every morning when you
wake, and every night before you go to
sleep. But you should learn to pray not
only at these regular times, but always
and everywhere; for you need God's help
and guidance all the day long, amidst
your tasks and pleasures, your troubles
and temptations. The life of Jesus was
always a life of prayer; the hands of
Jesus were always the hands of prayer.
And if you wish to be like Jesus you

also must learn to pray everywhere, lifting up holy hands to God.

3. The hands of Jesus were *helping hands.*

Wherever He went His hands were stretched out to help others. I am sure that when He was a little boy He helped His mother in the house, just as afterwards He helped Joseph in the shop. And when He began the great work of His public life, you know how many gracious and kindly acts the hands of Jesus performed. When the hungry came to Him, He gave them bread. When the blind came, He laid His fingers on their eyeballs and made them see. One day He went into a house where a little girl was lying cold and dead. But Jesus took her cold little hand into His strong living one, and said, "Damsel, I say unto thee, Arise!" and at once her spirit came back again, and she arose and walked. You cannot do such wonderful things as were done by the hands of Jesus; and yet how much even your hands can do to help others if only you are willing. What a help some girls are to their mothers, and some boys to their fathers. And how beautiful it is to see a child whose hands are helping hands, as the hands of Jesus were.

4. In the last place the hands of Jesus were *piercèd hands*.

That was what Jesus wanted His disciples to notice when He said, "Behold My hands." The disciples could not believe that this was actually Jesus risen from the dead, and so He showed them His hands and His feet, still pierced by the cruel nails with which He had been fastened to the cross.

Yes, the hands of Jesus were pierced hands; and Jesus wants us all to look at them, and to think why it was that the nails were driven through them. Don't you all know the reason why? It was

because Jesus loved us, and was willing
to lay down His life for our sakes, that
He suffered on that cross of Calvary.
"He was wounded for our transgressions,
and bruised for our iniquities." He died
to save us from our sins, and to win a
place for us in His Father's kingdom.
You remember the words of a beautiful
hymn in your own hymn-book :—

"How loving is Jesus who came from the sky,
　In tenderest pity for sinners to die ;
　His hands and His feet they were nailed to the
　　tree ;
　And all this He suffered for sinners like me."

Well, if Jesus did all this for you, what
should you do for Jesus? The hymn
goes on to tell you :—

"Oh, give then to Jesus your earliest days ;
　They only are blessed who walk in His ways ;
　In life and in death He will still be their Friend,
　For those whom He loves, He will love to the
　　end."

Loving though we cannot See.

———————

"Whom having not seen, ye love."—I PET. i. 8.

I WAS preaching lately in a church where the organist is blind. He was born blind, so that he never saw the trees and the hills and the sky; he never even saw his father's and mother's faces. He never saw an organ or a music-book; and yet he can play beautifully, and he loves to play, as may be seen from the light that comes into his face when he is playing. Many of you are learning music just now, and you know how much you depend at first upon your eyes. You have to look at the keys, so as to learn their names; and at the notes in the book, so as to know what keys to strike; and at those troublesome figures 1, 2, 3, 4, so as to know how to manage your fingers. I am sure you must wonder how it is possible for a blind boy ever to learn to play. And yet, because the blind lad I have told you of has some "music in his soul," and has also a sensitive ear and a delicate touch, he can play just as well as if he had perfect eyesight.

Now, sometimes people say that they cannot love Jesus Christ, because they cannot see Him. But we don't depend upon our eyes for loving Jesus any more than the blind organist depends upon his eyes for loving his organ. What Peter says about Jesus is true,—"Whom having not seen, ye love."

There are some boys and girls who lost their mother when they were babies. They don't remember anything about her; perhaps they never saw her at all. But their father sometimes speaks about her, and their elder sister tells them how good and kind she was; and often they look at her picture on the wall, and think about her, and wish she was with them still. And as they do this, they get to love her very much, although they have never seen her.

Well, it is something like that between our souls and Jesus. We have never seen Him; but we love Him, because He has first loved us, and because we have heard a great deal about His goodness and His love.

There was an old minister in Edinburgh whom I used to know, who had a blind boy in his congregation. One breezy day when the minister was out for a walk, he came upon this blind boy, all by himself on the hillside, flying a kite. He was sitting on the grass holding the string in his hand, and the kite was high up in the air. "What are you doing, James?" asked the minister. "I'm fleein' my drāgon," said the boy. "But you can't see it." "Oh no," he said, "I canna see it; but I can feel it aye tug-tuggin'." Well, there is just such a link between our souls and Jesus. We cannot see Him; but we can feel Him "aye tug-tuggin'," like the blind boy's invisible kite.

Sometimes Jesus "tugs" us through our consciences. Have you ever felt Jesus tugging at your conscience? Have you been tempted to do something wrong, and felt just then a strange feeling inside of you, as if some strong hand were pulling at your very heart-strings and saying, "Don't do it! Don't do it!"? That was Jesus tugging at your conscience. You could not see Him; but you felt His power.

Sometimes Jesus "tugs" us through our Christian faith and love. When we are sitting in church or Sabbath school on the Lord's own day, and hear about the Saviour's grace and goodness, we feel sorry to think how bad we have been, and we wish that we were much better than we are. And when children hear about the love of Jesus, and how He took the children in His arms and blessed them, and for their sakes died at last upon the cross, they cannot help loving Him, although they have never seen Him.

And sometimes Jesus "tugs" at our hearts in another way still. For amidst all our work and play, our pleasures and duties, we are apt to forget Him altogether. But He comes into our homes and takes away a child whom we dearly love. The little coffin is carried to the cemetery, and buried underneath the ground; but the little spirit has gone to be with Jesus. And when a father and

mother have a little child in heaven, and
when boys and girls have a brother or
sister there, that makes them think of
Jesus more than they used to do before.
For where our treasure is, there will our
heart be also.   And thus Jesus gets His
hand upon our heart-strings, and draws
our thoughts upwards, and teaches us
to set our affections upon the things
above.   And many a time we learn to
love Jesus just because He is the Good
Shepherd who takes care of our little
lambs.

So we do not need to see Jesus in
order to love Him.   What the apostle
says is true,—" Whom having not seen,
ye love ; in whom, though now ye see
Him not, yet believing, ye rejoice with
joy unspeakable and full of glory."

A Lesson from a Railway Lamp.

"Among whom ye shine as lights in the world."—
PHIL. ii. 15.

THIS text speaks about shining; and it also tells us why we ought to shine, viz., "as lights in the world." Sometimes we wish to shine, not that we may give light to others, but only for the sake of the pleasure and comfort and glory which it brings to ourselves. A boy likes to shine in the football field, because it's nice to hear people say that he is a splendid runner, or that no one can kick the ball so far as he. Another boy wishes

C

to shine at school, because he would like
to be looked upon, and spoken about, as
the cleverest boy in the class.   And girls
are fond of shining too.   They like to be
admired for their looks, or their dress, or
their manners, or their accomplishments,
or any other good qualities they possess.

Well, these are ways of shining ; and I
don't say that there is anything positively
wrong in wishing to shine in some of these
ways, although the desire to do it certainly
brings with it many dangers and temptations.   But, at all events, there's a better
way of shining, and that is to shine as
lights in the world—to shine, not for our
own pleasure or our own glory, but in
order that we may give light to other
people, and try to make them happy and
good.

Let me tell you a story which I have
read about shining for the sake of others.*

---

* Rev. F. C. Spurr in *Christian World Pulpit*,
16th December 1891.

A gentleman was standing one winter evening on a railway platform waiting for a train. And as he had some time to wait, he strolled up and down the station, until he came to the lamp-room. It was a very bright, warm room, and one of those large four-wheeled barrows, which railway porters use for the purpose, was standing on the floor filled with freshly lighted lamps. There was a new lamp in the barrow which had never been lighted before. It had come from the shop that very morning. And just as the gentleman came up, the new lamp was saying, "Yes, this is what I call jolly. I always thought that railway lamps had a bad time of it, hung up in cold carriages—at least, so I have been told; but this warm bright comfortable room is what I didn't expect; anyhow, it's very nice." One or two old shabby lamps, that had seen a great deal of service, smiled at this, and one of them whispered to the other, "Let him alone; he will tell a different tale when he has been out on duty for a few nights."

Just then a porter came into the room whistling a tune, and in a minute or two he had wheeled the lamps out to the cold draughty platform. The new lamp shivered, and said, "What next, I wonder? Surely he won't put us into the cold carriages." But the next moment the porter seized the lamp and tossed it up into the air, and another porter on the top of the train caught it cleverly with both his hands, and pushed it into a hole in the roof of a third-class carriage. And then the guard blew his whistle, and the train moved away.

Next evening the gentleman was at the railway station again, and he went along to the lamp-room to learn more about the lamps. They were all there once more, the new lamp included. And just as he came up, the new lamp was saying, "Wasn't I disappointed when the porter put me into a third-class carriage—a new lamp, mind you, into a dirty third-class carriage! It made me quite ill at first, but when I looked down into the compartment, I saw a woman with a sick baby, and she looked up and said, 'I'm so glad they have given us a nice bright light for once, for now I can see baby's face.' Then a working man pulled a newspaper out of his pocket and said, 'Yes, so am I, for I can see to read the evening paper. They don't often give us such a good light as this.' And then I noticed in a corner a girl with very red eyes, as if she had been crying, and she said, 'I'm going home to see my mother who is very ill, perhaps dying, and I wanted so much to read the letter that my sister wrote about her; and now I shall be able to read it with this bright light.' And they all seemed so glad about my light," the new lamp went on to say, "that I quite forgot my disappointment, and I did try to shine my very best. And now

I am quite looking forward to going out again to-night ; for it's much better to help other people than to stay here and enjoy oneself."

That story is a parable, but all of you will understand what it means. It tells us that we should shine, not for our own pleasure merely, but to bring light and joy into other lives. You boys and girls can do this. Your lights may not be very big or bright, as yet ; but, at least, you can be like the little candles of which you have just been singing—each in your small corner shining in the night. Or you can be like the fireflies I used to see when I was a boy in the dark tropical woods, tiny little things, with lights far feebler than the smallest candle, and yet breaking up the night and making it beautiful. Will you all try to shine, to shine for Jesus, and so give light to others in this dark world?

Lions in the Way.

———➤•◄———

"The slothful man saith, There is a lion in the way; a lion is in the streets. As the door turneth upon his hinges, so doth the slothful upon his bed."—PROV. xxvi. 13, 14.

IT would be a dreadful thing, would it not, if there were lions in the woods about Cathcart, and if sometimes we even heard them roaring in the streets? You have seen pictures of lions, and read stories about them; and some of you have seen a real living lion in a menagerie; and so you know what a dreadful beast a lion is. If there really was a lion in the way, you would have

a very good excuse for not going to
school in the morning. But the lion
the text speaks about is not in the
streets at all; he is only in the sluggard's
fancy. The sluggard does not want to
get out of his bed in the morning. It
is too cold, he thinks, or it is too early,
or he has not had enough slumber; and
so he cries out, "I can't get up; there's
a lion in the way." But the real lion
is in his own heart, and the name of this
lion is *Sloth*.

"'Tis the voice of the sluggard, I heard him
    complain,
  'You have waked me too soon, I must slumber
    again.'
  As the door on its hinges, so he on his bed
  Turns his side, and his shoulders, and his
    sleepy head."

I wonder if you boys and girls know
anything about that lion which Solomon's
sluggard heard roaring in the street, as
he lay in his bed in the morning.

But it is not only the sluggard who

says, "There is a lion in the way."
Sometimes when you ought to be learning your lessons, you don't wish to learn
them. You would much rather be outside playing on the roads, or else curled
up on the sofa with an exciting story
book in your hand. And just then you
may hear a lion roaring. "Your lessons
are too hard," it seems to say; or, "You
are not in a mood for studying to-
night"; or, "What's the use of learning
all that rubbish the teacher gives you to
learn? It won't be of the least use to
you by-and-by." Can you tell me the
name of this lion? His name is *Idleness,*
and most of you have met him some
time or other.

Sometimes at night, after the gas is
lighted in the parlour, your mother wants
you to go for something into a dark
room upstairs. And then you think that
there is a lion in the dark room, or if
not a lion there's a man, or else a bogle,

or some other strange monster of your
imagination. But there is nothing dangerous in the room at all. The lion is in
your own heart, and the name of the
lion is *Cowardice.*

Some day your father wants to send
you out on an errand; and at once a
lion appears in the way. You are too
tired, or you were just going to do something else, or you can't be bothered going
out at all. Now this lion's real name is
nothing else than *Disobedience;* for if you
truly loved and honoured your father,
as you ought to do, you would never
think of being tired or being bothered,
but would gladly do anything to help
him or to please him.

And here is another kind of lion that
often meets boys and girls in the way.
Their Sabbath School teacher has been
speaking to them about the love of Jesus
Christ, and telling them that Jesus wants
them to give their hearts to Him just

now, and to speak and act always like the friends of Jesus. But the children have caught sight of the lion. "Oh!" they say, "we are too young to be Christians. There will be plenty of time by-and-by. It's only grown-up people who can be proper Christians." I wonder if you can tell me the name of this lion that stands in the way. He has a very long name, for he is called *Procrastination*. And he has done a great deal of harm in the world to men and women, and boys and girls. A very greedy and devouring lion is *Procrastination*. He is often called "the thief of time"; but he is also the thief of souls.

But now I must tell you in closing that there is a more dangerous lion than any I have yet mentioned, and against him you should be on your special guard. The apostle Peter tells us that "the devil, as a roaring lion, walketh about, seeking whom he may devour." And the worst of it is that, instead of being frightened of this terrible lion, we often think that he is as harmless as a lamb; and so we let him walk down the street with us, and go into the playground with us, and come into the house and sit down beside us at the fireside. Sometimes in a menagerie there's a man called "the lion-tamer," who puts his head into the lion's mouth. It's a very dangerous thing to do; but it's just what some people do with this great roaring lion. They think he is quite tame, and they rather like his company; but some day, when it is too late, they find out their mistake.

Now it is this cunning old lion who sends all the other lions I have mentioned into your heads and hearts,— *Sloth*, and *Idleness*, and *Cowardice*, and *Disobedience*, and *Procrastination*. And so you must fight against him first of all, and most of all. "Whom resist," the apostle says, "stedfast in your faith."

Ask Jesus to help you, and He will clothe you with His heavenly armour, and fill you with His Holy Spirit. And then, children though you are, you shall be stronger than this great lion, and all the other lions as well ; for you shall be more than conquerors through Him that loved you.

The Yoke of Christ.

"Take My yoke upon you."—MATT. xi. 29.

ONE Sabbath morning not long ago I spoke to the older folks about the time in Christ's life when He was the Carpenter of Nazareth. Do you boys ever think of Jesus as a carpenter? I remember when I was a little boy that we went to live in a new house before it was quite finished, and there was a carpenter who stayed and worked about the house for several weeks. Not long before I had learned that Jesus was a carpenter, and this gave me a great reverence for this man. I used to stand beside him, and watch him sawing boards lengthwise and crosswise; or smoothing them with his plane until the ground was all covered with curly shavings; and I thought that Jesus when He was working must have looked exactly like that. Whilst he was still employed about the house, my little brother fell sick and died, and it was this carpenter who made his coffin. I remember to this day how I stood beside him, watching and wondering, while he made the little coffin out of sweet-smelling cedar wood. And this made me think more than ever that this carpenter must be like Jesus; for it was Jesus, I knew, who had taken my brother away.

Jesus was a carpenter. But what kind of work did Jesus do? Most of His work would be done for the people who lived in the town of Nazareth. But sometimes, perhaps, He made articles for the farmers who lived outside of the town; and when He worked for them, He would make ploughs (for ploughs were made of wood in those days), and carts, and yokes for the oxen.

A great Russian artist * has painted a picture of Jesus the Carpenter. He represents Jesus as seated in His workshop with a yoke upon His knees, to which He is just giving the last touches; and as He bends over His task there is a look of profound thought upon His face, which is meant to show that whilst He was fashioning this yoke He was thinking all the time of another yoke which He would make, not for oxen, but for men; and how He would invite all the weary and the heavy laden to take *His* yoke upon them, and so find rest unto their souls.

I wonder if you boys and girls know

---

* Verestchagin.

what is meant by the yoke of Christ. Perhaps you think that it is some disagreeable and painful thing that Jesus wants you to bear. If so you are making a great mistake. Christ's yoke is meant to make your life easier and happier, not to make it harder and more burdensome. The farmers in Palestine put yokes upon their oxen, not to make their burdens heavier, but to make them lighter. If the oxen had tried to draw the cart or the plough without a yoke, they would soon have been lamed or strangled. But they went along quite easily and lightly when they had the yoke upon their shoulders.

Now men, and women, and boys, and girls have all got burdens to bear, and they need a yoke of some kind to enable them to bear these burdens. Jesus knows this, and He wants us to take *His* yoke, because that yoke is the best. "Take *My* yoke," He says. "Don't take any

D

other yoke. Take *My* yoke upon you and learn of Me; and ye shall find rest unto your souls."

I wonder if I could guess the names of any of the burdens which boys and girls have to bear. One burden is the burden of work. There is your school work, for example. It must be done; but sometimes young people don't like very much to do it. How then are you to get it done? Perhaps you take upon you the yoke of fear. You say, "If I don't do it I shall be punished." Or else you take the yoke of ambition. You say, "If I do it, and do it well, I may get a prize." But how poor such yokes are in comparison with the yoke of Christ! Do your work for Jesus' sake, because you want to be a scholar in His school, and to learn of Him, and to please Him; and then your tasks will be easy, and your burden will be light.

If there was time I might speak of some

of your other burdens. I might tell you about a child's sorrows, and a child's temptations, and a child's sins. To get relief from the weight of all these burdens you need to have a yoke. Many yokes may be tried; but there is no yoke like the yoke of Christ. And so you must come to Jesus with all your sorrows, and temptations, and sins, if you want to find rest unto your souls.

I can fancy that, in the days when Jesus was a carpenter, there were other carpenters in Galilee who made yokes too, and sold them to the farmers. But there were no yokes like those which were made by the Carpenter of Nazareth. His yokes never pinched the necks of the oxen, and never galled their shoulders; they always fitted easily and perfectly, and so made the burdens light.

Now Christ's yoke for you is just like that. Don't go to anybody else for relief from your burdens; but come to Jesus first of all. Listen even now to this gracious invitation : — " Take My yoke upon you, and learn of Me ; for I am meek and lowly in heart ; and ye shall find rest unto your souls."

God's Library.

"In Thy book all my members were written."—
Ps. cxxxix. 16.

"Put Thou my tears into Thy bottle : are they
not in Thy book?"—Ps. lvi. 8.

"And the books were opened."—REV. xx. 12.

"The Lamb's book of life."—REV. xxi. 27.

"GOD'S Library!" I hear you say; "what does the minister mean by that?" Perhaps some of you will guess that by God's Library I mean the Bible. The Bible is made up of sixty-six different books, and though all of these books were written by men, they were written at the same time by the special help of God's Spirit. And so

these sixty-six. books are justly spoken
of as God's books, and one of the Fathers
of the Church, who lived many centuries
ago, called the Bible, as a whole, " The
Divine Library."

But it is not the Bible that I am
thinking of at present. All of you have
seen that library; but the library I wish
to tell you about is one which no eye
but God's has ever seen. God writes with
His own hand the books of which it is
composed, and He keeps those books in
His own keeping. And yet those invisible
books are full of interest to us; for while
God alone is the author of them, it is
about us that He writes,—about you and
me, and all the men and women and
children in the world. What a wonderful
library God's library must be; and how
wonderful too to think that your name
and mine should be written on the pages
of those invisible books in the library of
God. Let me tell you of four of those

strange books of God which are mentioned in the Bible.

1. *The book of our members :*—" In Thy book all my members were written."

Our members are just the various parts of our body—hands and feet, head and heart, eyes and ears. Well, God has written down all these members in one of His wonderful books. He knows all about them. It was He who made them, and nothing can happen to any one of them without His seeing it and marking it down. "He keepeth all our bones," says a psalmist, "not one of them is broken." And Jesus Himself tells us that even the very hairs of our head are all numbered. And God knows at every moment what all our members are after. He watches where our feet are going and what our hands are doing. He listens to the words that fall from our mouths, and He marks the very glances that shoot from our eyes.

Shouldn't we be very glad to think that God is watching so lovingly over all our members, even the smallest? And shouldn't we also be very careful that none of these members should do anything that would vex our loving and watchful heavenly Father? Remember the great purpose for which each and all of your members were given :—

> " Two little eyes to look to God ;
> Two little ears to hear His word ;
> Two little feet to walk in His ways ;
> One little mouth to sing His praise ;
> Two little hands to do His will ;
> And one little heart to love Him still."

2. *The book of our tears :—*" Put Thou my tears into Thy bottle: are they not in Thy book ? "

God not only writes about our members; He notes our feelings ; He marks every tear that we shed. Sometimes a child thinks that no one knows its sorrows. Perhaps your mother is not near, and there is nobody to whom you can tell the trouble of your heart. But God knows. He marks the poor little sparrow that falls to the ground; and much more will He mark the tears of a little child. Think of that, you who are unkind and cruel to the little ones, you who make the bitter tears roll down their cheeks. God is watching. God knows what you have done. He has written those tears in His book; and He will make you suffer for your cruelty to the little children whom He loves.

3. *The book of judgment:*—" The dead were judged out of those things which were written in the books."

In the days of the Inquisition, long ago, a prisoner was brought before a court. The lawyers were cross-examining him, and he was answering their questions very freely. But suddenly he heard, from behind a curtain, the sound of a pen scratching, scratching very fast;

and with that he grew silent, and refused to answer; for he knew that his words were being taken down, and that for every word he spoke he would have to give account.

And there is some One behind the curtain, some One whom you cannot see, who is writing down everything you say and think and do.

> "For we know the Lord of glory
>   Always sees what children do,
>   And is writing now the story
>   Of their thoughts and actions too."

Be careful, children! Think of that great day when the books shall be opened, and the dead shall be judged out of those things which are written in the books.

4. *The Lamb's book of life.*

Of all the books in God's library this is the most precious and the most wonderful. The Lamb is Jesus Christ the Son of God. He is called the Lamb, because He offered up Himself as a sacrifice for our sins, and because we are "redeemed with the precious blood of Christ, as of a lamb without blemish and without spot." And the Lamb's book of life is the book in which are written the names of all those to whom Jesus has given eternal life, those who shall pass through the gates into the heavenly city, and shall "eat of the tree of life, which is in the midst of the paradise of God."

What would we not give to have a peep into that book, and to see that our names are written there? But the book is shut and sealed; and no one as yet can look into it, except God Himself and Jesus Christ His Son. And yet, without looking into the book, it is possible for us to know that our names are written there. For all who trust in Jesus as their Saviour, and love Him as their Friend, and seek to "follow the Lamb whithersoever He goeth," may be sure that their names are in the Lamb's book of life. Will you not give your hearts to Jesus, so that you may know that your names are inscribed in this wonderful book, and that in the great day, when the book of life is opened, Jesus will confess your name before His Father and before His angels?

God's Hammer.

"Is not My word, saith the Lord, like a hammer that breaketh the rock in pieces?"—JER. xxiii. 29.

I WONDER if you have ever noticed, in reading the Bible, how many different things there are to which God's Word is compared. It is called a lamp and a looking-glass; it is called a shield and a sword; it is likened to seed which the sower casts into the furrows; to milk which is given to new-born babes; and in this text to a hammer which breaks the rock in pieces. Perhaps I may tell you, by-and-by, of some of the other things to which God's Word is compared ; but this morning let me speak to you of God's Word as a hammer.

There are two chief ways, I think, in which all of you have seen a hammer used. Sometimes when you are out for a walk you see a man who wears a curious pair of spectacles standing by the wayside with a heap of stones lying before him. The stones are big hard lumps of rock, and he wants to break them down into little pieces, so that they may be used to mend the roads. But how is he ever to do it? Well, see, in his hand he holds a heavy hammer, and with that hammer he strikes and strikes until the big lumps of stone have all been broken down into those little fragments which are called road metal, and which are used for mending rough and muddy roads. That is one great use of a hammer—it is used to break things down.

But, again, if you watch a house that is

being built, you see the joiners working away with planks and boards. And how do they get these planks and boards to stay in their proper places, so as not to tumble down? See, again, they have hammers in their hands; and with these hammers they drive nails into the roof and walls and floor, until every board and plank is firmly fastened in its proper place. That is another use of a hammer—not to break down, but to build up.

Now, God's Word is like both of these kinds of hammer, the stonebreaker's hammer, and the joiner's hammer. It can break things down, and it can also build things up.

1. *It is a hammer which breaks down everything that is bad.* You have all heard of Martin Luther, the famous monk who shook the world. And how did he shake the world? It was with the hammer of God's Word. The Pope of Rome had persuaded men to believe a great many

false and foolish things that were doing great harm to their souls; but Luther came with the Bible hammer, and broke all that rubbish down.

If you are ever tempted to do something that is wrong, just take the Bible hammer in your hand, and it will break the bad temptations in pieces. Perhaps you feel inclined to take something that is not your own; but down comes this hammer with a heavy blow, saying, "Thou shalt not steal." Perhaps you are tempted to tell a lie; down it comes again, and says, "Lying lips are an abomination to the Lord." Some day a dreadful noise is heard in the parlour where the children are playing. Tom and his brother have come to blows, and are knocking over the parlour chairs in all directions. Or two of the girls are quarrelling about a doll, or are both trying to get possession of the piano at the same time. And in the midst of all this strife down comes the Bible hammer with a tremendous blow, saying, "Little children, love one another."

2. But God's hammer *not only breaks down what is bad, but builds up what is good.* God wants our souls to be built up into beautiful temples; and God's Word is a hammer which enables us in the building of this temple to fasten everything in its proper place. Here, for example, is a plank called faith. Without faith the temple cannot be built; but, unless we have in our hands the hammer of God's Word, our faith can never be secure. Here is another plank called love; but it is only by God's hammer that that plank can be fastened for ever to the walls of the heart. Here is another plank called obedience; and down comes the hammer with a rap, rap, rap on the heart of every child, saying, "Honour thy father and thy mother;" and so that plank is fastened too. And it is just the same with everything else that is pure and lovely and good. It

E

is by the help of the hammer of God's Word that these things are built up into our lives.

I met a little boy the other day who told me that when he grows up he means to be a joiner. I wish you would all be joiners in my sense of the word, and little stonebreakers too. Get a firm hold of God's hammer, and try to break down everything that is bad, and to build up everything that is good.

God's Looking=Glass.

———————

"For if any be a hearer of the Word, and not a doer, he is like unto a man beholding his natural face in a glass."—JAMES i. 23.

"Beholding as in a glass the glory of the Lord."—2 COR. iii. 18.

I SPOKE to you lately about God's hammer, *i.e.*, the hammer of God's Word. And I was glad, since that, to meet a boy who said that he was going to keep hold of that wonderful hammer, and try to use it every day.

But this morning I wish to speak to you about God's looking-glass; for that is another of the names by which God's Word is described. You all know the use of a looking-glass. It is for looking at ourselves in, and seeing what we are like. If you are going to a party, and want to be perfectly neat and tidy, you look into the glass before you go out, in case any stain should be on your face, or your hair should not be quite smooth, or your collar not quite straight. The looking-glass shows you exactly what you are like; and, in another sense, that is just what the Bible does too. We look into God's Word, and there we behold our " natural face as in a glass."

Sometimes little girls, I have been told, like to look into the mirror, because they think they are pretty, and they like to see their own sweet faces. But no one who looks into God's looking-glass can ever think that he or she is beautiful. This mirror does not flatter us, it makes us appear quite ugly, and vile, and sinful.

Perhaps you have got your hands and

face freshly washed, and your hair smoothly brushed, and a clean collar on. If you look into the bedroom looking-glass, you think you are as nice as nice can be. But take a peep into God's looking-glass, and you see things quite differently. Your face is ugly, because it was screwed up this morning in anger and passion. Your mouth is dirty, because only a little while ago you spoke rudely and disobediently to your mother. And your hands are as black as a sweep's, because those newly washed hands are the very hands that slapped your little sister and made her cry, and went into the press when no one was looking, and took something there that didn't belong to you.

The Bible, you see, is not a very pleasant looking-glass in which to see ourselves, because it never flatters us, but always shows us how bad and sinful we are.

But there is something else we see in God's looking-glass besides our own faces. Sometimes when you look into a glass you do not see your own face at all, because you are not standing just in front of it; but you see your mother's face or your sister's face in another part of the room. And when we look into the Bible looking-glass it is not always ourselves that we see. We see the face of Jesus Christ. We behold "as in a glass the glory of the Lord." And oh, what a beautiful face the face of Jesus is! There is no stain of sin upon it. There is no mark of selfishness and passion. There is nothing in *His* face but goodness, and kindness, and love.

Now, I want you to look into the Bible looking-glass, so as to see both of these faces side by side,—your own face and the face of Jesus; just as you might stand in front of a mirror, and see yourself there, with your mother looking over your shoulder. And remember this, that if God's mirror shows your face to be soiled and ugly, Jesus Christ can make it pure and beautiful. By looking at Jesus, and loving Jesus, your face may grow into the likeness of His own. "Beholding as in a glass the glory of the Lord, we are changed into the same image from glory to glory." Is not God's Word a wonderful mirror, when it has a transforming power like that? Will you not prize this precious looking-glass which God has put into your hands, and use it every day you live; so that you may see your natural face in all its need of cleansing, but may also see that gracious Saviour who can take all your sins away, and put His own holy beauty into your faces as well as your hearts?

God's Search=Light.

———•—•—•———

"Search me, O God, and know my heart; try me, and know my thoughts."—Ps. cxxxix. 23.

THIS verse speaks about an examination. But there are different kinds of examinations. Those of you who are attending the public schools are quite familiar with one kind of examination. Every year Her Majesty's Inspector comes round to examine the school. He searches it, and tries it, to see if the teachers have been teaching well, and if the scholars have been learning well. That is one kind of examination — an examination of your minds.

And some of you have had to pass through another kind of examination. One morning when you woke you felt all out of sorts. Your mother said that you must not rise from your bed; and she sent a messenger to ask the doctor to come and see you. When the doctor came he felt your pulse, and made you show him your tongue ; and after that he took a little thermometer out of his pocket, and put it under your arm, and then looked at it after a while, to see what he called your temperature, and to know whether or not you were in a fever. That was a quite different examination from the school inspector's—an examination of your body.

But the text speaks of a different examination still—an examination of the heart. " Search me, O God, and know my heart ; try me, and know my thoughts."

An inspector can examine your minds, a doctor can examine your bodies, but God alone can truly examine your hearts. Only God can tell what thoughts, and feelings, and desires are passing through you at this very moment; only God can see the selfishness, and pride, and anger, and hatred that lurk continually within you, in those deep places of the soul to which your neighbours' eyes can never reach. Our hearts are very dark, as dark as night; but God can see right into them, and God can enable us to see into them ourselves.

I was once staying in a little village far up a long fiord on the west coast of Norway. It was late at night, and I had gone out to take a stroll before going to bed. It was darker than usual that night, and nothing could be seen except the black masses of the mountains against the sky, with the pale glimmer of the ice and snow lying on their broad summits.

But all at once a great sheet of light seemed to fall just where I stood, and everything round about was as distinctly seen as if it had been the middle of the day. The light travelled along the shore until the houses at a distance, and the startled men and women who came running out of doors, were just as plain as sunlight could have made them. Then it crept up the mountain side, and every boulder and pine tree stood out in sharp distinction from its neighbour. At last, before it disappeared, it flashed upon the snow and ice of the great glacier, that crowned the mountains, almost dazzling one's eyes with the shining whiteness.

Perhaps some of you have guessed already what that strange light was. It was a *search-light*, and it came from a large steamer that lay out on the fiord. A search-light is a very powerful electric light which is carried by men-of-war and some other vessels, and which enables them to see by night as well as by day. Now God can cast a search-light of His own upon our hearts, and though our hearts are very dark and full of hidden things, God can make all these hidden things perfectly plain.

God has a search-light which He calls *conscience.* Sometimes He turns it on in all its power, and it makes us feel very uncomfortable and miserable, as we see what bad and ugly things are lurking within us. And God has another search-light which He calls *the Bible.* It also can reveal all hidden things, yea, the very thoughts and intents of the heart. Have you not sometimes felt as you read the Bible that God knows all about you, and that God is also enabling you to see yourselves as you really are? Once when I was visiting at a farmhouse that stands on the edge of an Ayrshire moor, the farmer's wife told me that they were reading just then through the Book of Proverbs at family worship, and that the servant girl said to her one day, " I dinna like yon book ; it kens ower muckle about folk." Yes, sometimes it is not very pleasant to have the search-light turned on. But it is good for us. The inspector examines the school, not because he wants to find fault, or wants to make you fail, but because he wants to make you better scholars than you are. The doctor examines you when you are ill, not because he wants to hurt you, but because he wants to make you well. And God searches us, and tries us, in order to make us better boys and better girls, better men and better women.

That was why the Psalmist wished God to search him ; so that if there was any wicked way in him, God might reveal it, and might lead him in the way ever-lasting. Will you not take his prayer and make it your own ? Ask God to show you what is wrong and wicked in your hearts and lives; and to lead you with His strong hand in His own ever-lasting way.

The Lily and the Cedar.

"I will be as the dew unto Israel: he shall grow as the lily, and cast forth his roots as Lebanon."—HOSEA xiv. 5.

YOU could hardly imagine two kinds of growth more different from each other than the tiny lily, and the great cedar tree which casts forth its roots on the slopes of Mount Lebanon. But both of them are planted by the same divine hand, and both of them are watered by the same heavenly dew.

Let me tell you a story about a cedar
and a lily that grew on the heights of
Lebanon long ago.   It was in the days of
King Solomon, a thousand years before
Jesus Christ was born in Bethlehem.
Great bands of wood-cutters were on the
mountain, cutting down cedars for the
building of the temple at Jerusalem.
And at noon-tide, when all the foresters
were resting for a while, there was one
of them who threw himself down under
the shadow of a great cedar tree, not far
from where a beautiful lily was growing
amidst the grass.   I cannot tell you
whether or not he fell asleep as he lay
there and rested; at all events he heard
by-and-by the sound of a gentle voice;
and, as he listened, he found that it was
the lily who was speaking.   And this
was what the lily said :—

"O great cedar tree, I wish that I
were you!   I am so weak and helpless;
but you are so great and strong.   I am

so small that I can hardly see above the grass; but you are so tall that you can see away down the valley, as far as the peaks of the distant mountains And I am very useless too. I can do nothing to help anybody. But you give the birds room to build their nests in your branches, and here is this tired wood-cutter enjoying a rest in your deep shade. And, besides, I heard the king's officer saying to-day to the woodmen that you are to be taken away to Jerusalem, to be made into a beautiful pillar in the temple of God, carved all over with lovely figures, and covered with yellow gold. How I wish that I could be great and strong and useful like you!"

Then the woodman heard a sound like the wind rustling in the branches overhead; but it was the cedar giving a melancholy sigh. "Lily of the valley," it said, "do not envy me. Your lot, I

F

am sure, is far happier than mine. I
have no delicate beauty like you, no
sweet fragrant smell. I am a gnarled
old cedar tree. The storms shake and
toss my branches, while they leave you
lying peacefully on the ground. And
then, as you have said, I am going to
be cut down, and dragged away to the
foot of the mountain, and carried to
Jerusalem. It may be that I shall be
turned into a pillar in this great temple
they are building; but I would much
rather stay where I am on the mountain
side. I wish I were, like you, a humble
lily of the valley, with no battles to
fight, and no troubles to vex me."

When the woodman heard this, he
could be silent no longer, but said—

"Listen to me, O cedar tree, and lily
of the valley. Has not God planted
both of you, has He not caused you both
to grow, has He not watered you alike
with His own dew, and has He not given

to each of you your own proper work
to do? The cedar has made Lebanon
beautiful from afar; it has welcomed
the birds to its shelter, it has guarded
the lily from the tempest, it has given
me a shadow in the heat. And now it
is going to Jerusalem to glorify the
house of God's glory. But the lily also
has been filling a place that nothing else
could have filled. The wild bees have
sucked honey from its bending cup, the
wood-cutters have enjoyed its beauty
and its fragrance, and it has made them
think of the love of the great God who
cares for the lilies of the field."

Now, children, you sometimes feel like
that lily, do you not? You think that
if you were great and wise and strong,
your lives might be happier and better
than they are. But remember that older
people also have their troubles and diffi-
culties. And remember too that God
made the lilies as well as the cedars

and that He has plenty of work for the lilies to do. Seek to glorify God in the place where He has planted you. Be pure and sweet and fragrant like a lily of the valley; and then your lives will be full of happiness, and full of usefulness as well.

There was a great poet called Ben Jonson, who lived in England long ago. He wrote many famous works, but he never wrote anything more beautiful than these lines, which tell us how a little child may glorify God :—

> "It is not growing like a tree
>   In bulk, doth make man better be ;
> Or standing long an oak three hundred year,
> To fall a log at last, dry, bald, and sere :
>   A lily of a day
>   Is fairer far in May ;
>   Although it fall and die that night,
>   It was the plant and flower of light.
> In small proportions we just beauty see ;
> And in short measures life may perfect be."

Try to remember that. A life of small

proportions may be a life of true beauty and perfection. For God loves the children, and **God** has something on earth for the children to do.

The Message of the Bridge.

"Come unto Me, all ye that labour and are heavy laden, and I will give you rest."—·MATT. xi. 28.

THERE is a town in Austria which is built, like Glasgow, on two sides of a large river. And there is a bridge, corresponding to Glasgow Bridge, which connects the two parts of the town. A great many people have to cross this bridge every day—workmen going to their work, and merchants going to business, and children going to school, and message-boys sent out on errands.

And on the panels of the bridge a sculptor has carved with a loving hand many of the most familiar scenes from the life of Jesus Christ; so that, day by day, all who cross the river may find something to teach them, or something to comfort, or something to strengthen, or something to save, if they will but glance at the sculptures on the bridge as they pass by.

If a man passes who has done something very wrong, but who is sorry for it, he may see Jesus in the Pharisee's house saying to the penitent woman, " Thy sins be forgiven thee." If a funeral passes over, and the mourners are feeling very sad, they have only to look at the bridge, and they will see Jesus comforting Martha, and saying to her, " I am the Resurrection and the Life." If a little child goes over, and looks at all the pictures, one by one, as a child would be apt to do, he will come, by-and-by, to one that he will like the best—Jesus taking the young children in

His arms and blessing them, while He says, "Suffer the little children to come unto Me, and forbid them not ; for of such is the kingdom of God."

Now, I think that that old bridge preaches a far better sermon to children on the subject of my text than I could possibly preach. Shakespeare tells us about "sermons in stones," and that bridge is just a sermon in stone. Every day it says to all who pass by, "Come to Jesus! Come to Jesus! Come unto Me, all ye that labour and are heavy laden, and I will give you rest."

Let me tell you, very shortly, of three great burdens from which Jesus will give you rest.

1. One is the burden of *sin.*

That's the worst burden of all. Don't you know something about it, dear children? Haven't you sometimes felt a heavy load lying upon your heart, because you have done what is wrong, or because, even when you were trying to do what was right, evil thoughts and angry passions *would* arise? Well, take that burden to Jesus. Ask Him to forgive your sins, and He will do it. Ask Him to keep evil thoughts and angry passions from arising in your heart, and Jesus will do that too.

2. Another burden is the burden of *duty*.

Sometimes boys and girls, just like men and women, feel the burden of duty to be heavy and irksome. Perhaps you don't like to learn your lessons for the school; perhaps you don't like to let your brothers and sisters have any of their own way; perhaps you don't like to do what father and mother tell you. These duties, you think, are all very hard. Well, why not take your load to Jesus, and ask Him to give you rest? He will help you to like duties that seem to be unpleasant, and so your yoke will be easy, and your burden will be light.

3. The last burden is the burden of
sorrow.

We older people are apt to think that
you boys and girls have got no experience
of sorrow. You seem so happy, for the
most part, that we sometimes wish we
were young again, just as you are now.
But I know that children have their
sorrows too. Your hearts are sometimes
vexed and pained, and the tears come
starting into your eyes. Well, Jesus can
take the pain out of your hearts, and He
can wipe away the tears from your eyes.
Jesus is always sorry when He sees a child
crying, and if you would only listen at
such a time, you might hear Him saying,
"Come unto Me, and I will give you rest."
Try to get into the way of telling Jesus
about all your sorrows, the little sorrows
as well as the big ones, and you will find
that it brings a wonderful relief, and gives
"rest unto your souls."

Stephen's Three Crowns.

"And they stoned Stephen, calling upon God, and saying, Lord Jesus, receive my spirit."—ACTS vii. 59.

MANY of you know that Stephen was the first of all the Christian martyrs, the first of that long line of heroic men and women, yes, and of heroic boys and girls as well, who laid down their lives for the sake of Jesus Christ. We are not told a great deal about Stephen in the book of *Acts*; but what we are told is very interesting and very touching. Perhaps I might sum up the whole of his history in these three statements. First, he was "a good man." Next, this good man was stoned to death for the sake of Jesus Christ. And lastly, Christ gave His martyred servant a glorious reward. For Stephen "fell asleep" in Jesus; while his face shone, like the face of an angel, with the light of that great glory into which he was about to pass.

Now, I think I might put these three things which I have told you about Stephen, into a form which you would more easily remember. Let us think of them as three crowns which Stephen wore. Stephen is a Greek name; and in Greek Stephen, or Στέφανος, means "a crown." And this man, whose very name means a crown, had three shining crowns set upon his brow—first, the crown of grace; next, the crown of thorns; and lastly, the crown of glory.

1. Stephen's first crown was *the crown of grace.*

Grace is just another name for goodness. It means a goodness which is so pure and beautiful that we know at once that it must be the gift of God. And Stephen was a man on whose head God had set this "ornament of grace." We are told that he was "a good man, full of faith and of the Holy Ghost." And we can see for ourselves how full of grace he must have been, when we read the speech that he made to his judges, and still more when we see the way in which he died. For what a wonderful death it was that Stephen died, kneeling down and praying to God, and crying with his last breath, "Lord, lay not this sin to their charge."

Surely it was nothing but that "grace of the Lord Jesus Christ" with which Stephen had been so abundantly crowned, that could have enabled him to die in such a fashion, praying, even as Christ had prayed upon the cross, that his cruel murderers should be forgiven.

2. Stephen's second crown was *the crown of thorns.*

You remember that when Jesus was led away to Calvary, He had a crown of thorns upon His brow. What a painful thing it must have been to have those great sharp thorns piercing into His flesh, and making the blood run down His face! And so the crown of thorns has become a symbol for the sore suffering which a Christian sometimes has to bear, as he seeks to walk in his Master's footsteps. Stephen's suffering was of a very dreadful kind. He was stoned with great stones, until all the life was quite beaten out of his body. And he suffered this torture for Jesus' sake, because he loved Jesus so well that he would not deny his Lord, or cease to proclaim His truth, even though a horrible death was staring him in the face. There were multitudes of martyrs, by-and-by, who wore for Jesus' sake the crown of thorns and suffering. But

Stephen's crown shines before us with a special brightness, because he was the first of all the Christian martyrs.

3. Stephen's third crown was *the crown of glory.*

He "fell asleep"; but it was to awake in a glorious world, and a still more glorious presence. Just before they began to stone him, he looked up to heaven, "and saw the glory of God, and Jesus standing at the right hand of God." Can we doubt what that vision meant? It was Jesus rising to greet His faithful servant, and to bestow upon him "a crown of glory that fadeth not away."

It was that splendid vision which filled Stephen with peace, and charity, and triumph, in the very midst of his suffering.

"He heeded not reviling tones,
  Nor sold his heart to idle moans,
  Tho' cursed and scorned, and bruised with stones:

But looking upward full of grace,
He prayed, and from a happy place
God's glory smote him on the face."

Now, dear young friends, would you
not like to wear two at least of Stephen's
crowns—the crown of grace, and the crown
of glory? I pray that God in His mercy
would spare you, as far as may be possible
and right, from thorns and sufferings;
and that if the crown of thorns should
come to you, He would give you strength
to bear it patiently for Jesus' sake. But,
at all events, will you not seek to have
the crown of grace on earth, and the
crown of glory in heaven?

There was once a boy who was the
eldest son of a well-known Scotch duke,
and who lay dying of consumption. His
minister came to see him, and the boy
took his Bible from beneath his pillow,
and opened it at the words, "I have
fought a good fight, I have finished my
course, I have kept the faith. Henceforth
there is laid up for me a crown of
righteousness, which the Lord, the right-
eous judge, shall give me at that day."

"This," he said, "is all my comfort." After that, as death drew nearer, he called his younger brother to his side, and bade him farewell; and then he said, "Now, Douglas, in a little while you will be a duke, but I shall be a king."

None of you will ever be a duke; but all of you may be something much better than that. You may be little kings and queens, crowned with crowns of grace even now, and heirs to crowns of glory by-and-by. Give yourselves to Jesus, as Stephen did, with a strong and loving faith; and Jesus will see to it that both here and hereafter you shall not lack His promised crowns.

Asking and Receiving.

"Ask, and it shall be given you."—MATT. vii. 7.

THIS is a text which all children can easily understand. For children are always asking for things, and they are continually getting things in answer to their requests. A little baby only a few days old knows how to ask. It cannot speak a single word; it has "no language but a cry." But how ready it is to cry, and how lustily it does cry once it begins. And what is a baby's cry but its way of asking? Sometimes that cry means, "I'm very hungry, please give me some food!" and sometimes it means, "I've got a dreadful pain, won't you do something to take the pain away?" And then, when a baby gets a little older, but is still unable to speak, it begins to ask by using its hands. If it sees a rosy-cheeked apple on the table, it stretches out its hands, as much as to say, "I want that apple!" If it is taken to the window on a moonlight night, and sees the moon shining in the sky, it will stretch its little hands upwards, and wriggle in its mother's arms, saying as plainly as it can, "Please give me the moon!" And when children grow older still, and get the free use of their tongues, they keep running to their mother all day long, and asking for things —a "piece," or a drink, or a picture-book, or a toy, or a pencil and paper to write imaginary letters, or something else that comes into their heads.

A child's daily life is a very good illustration of asking and receiving. And so we find that Jesus, in this same passage, takes the case of a little child asking his father for something, as an example of what we should all do when we go in prayer to our Father in heaven. A child, says Jesus, asks his father for bread or for fish, and the father grants the child's request. He does not give a stone instead of bread, or a serpent in place of a fish. And if men who are evil know how to give good gifts unto their children, much more will our Father in heaven give good things to them that ask Him.

Remember, then, boys and girls, that God is your Father in heaven, and that just as you go to your father and mother with your requests, so should you go to God. God loves you more than your mother does ; and God is far stronger and kinder than your father. Every day you should tell Him about all your troubles and all your wants. And be sure of this, that if your father and mother try to give you what you need much more will your heavenly Father give you all good things.

But does God always give us the very things for which we ask? "Ask, and it shall be given you," the text says. But this does not mean that God will do exactly what we ask. We must think again of that illustration which Jesus uses of a father and his little child.

There are some things which children ask, but which their parents do not give. A child's request is sometimes an impossible request. And there are other requests which, if they are not impossible, are yet so foolish that fathers and mothers cannot grant them. When your little brother was brought to the table for the first time, he immediately wanted to get hold of a knife. But your mother said, "No!" for she knew how dangerous that would be. When children are at the stage at which one of the chief

pleasures of life consists in eating sweeties,
they often wish to have far more sweet
things than would be good for them.
But their mother says, "No!" because
she does not want them to make themselves ill. A boy sometimes comes to
his father and asks to be allowed to go
to a certain place, or to do a certain
thing; but the father, who knows the
world much better than his boy, thinks
it would be safest and best not to give
permission, and therefore he says, "No!"

Well, God deals with us just as a wise
and loving parent does. There are some
prayers which are impossible prayers.
God could not grant them without con-
tradicting Himself, without turning upside
down those great laws by which He
governs the world. And there are some
prayers which are foolish prayers. Perhaps
we do not think so; but God knows
much better than we, and therefore God
says, "No!" A parent gives his child

"good things"; and our heavenly Father wants us only to have "good things," not things that are foolish or wrong.

"Ask, and it shall be given you." Will you boys and girls remember that? You do not hesitate to go to your father and mother with your requests, and you must not hesitate to go to God. If your request is a good one, God will grant it when you ask Him. Only you must ask in real earnest. You must mean what you say; and you must show that you mean it by your manner of asking. "Ask, and Seek, and Knock," the verse says; that is, don't ask once only, but go on asking, and ask more earnestly every time. Mr Moody once told this story at a children's meeting:—"Sometimes in the house my little boy will be playing, and he will stop and say, 'Papa, please give me a drink of water!' But if I am busy writing, and I see that he goes back to his play, I don't think he is very thirsty, and I don't rise to get it. Perhaps he comes once or twice and asks again ; but if he runs back to his play, I know that he does not want it very much. But by-and-by he gets thoroughly in earnest; he throws away his toys, and comes and seizes hold of my hand. He *must* have the water now, he is *so* thirsty. Then, of course, I go to get it, because I see that he really wants it." Even so, when we go to God and ask with heartfelt earnestness, God will give us all good things.

The Image of God.

———◆———

"The Image of the invisible God."—COL. i. 15.

WHEN visitors come to call at your house, some of you like very much to fetch the album, and point out the photographs of all your friends. "This is father," you say, "and this is mother, and this is Mary, and this is James, and this is me." By-and-by you come to another photograph further on, and you say, "This is my uncle in Australia." "But did you ever see this uncle in Australia?" your visitor asks. "Oh no!" you reply, "I never saw him, I've just heard father and mother speaking about him." And yet you know what he is like, you have a clear picture of him in your mind's eye, because you have so often looked at his image or portrait in the album.

Sometimes, again, when you have been in Glasgow, you have passed through George Square. And in the Square you have seen a great many statues or images standing on high pedestals. One is the statue of James Watt, the inventor of the steam-engine; another of Sir Walter Scott, the author of "Rob Roy," and "Ivanhoe," and many more splendid stories; another of Robert Burns, the Ayrshire ploughman who became Scotland's greatest poet; and another of David Livingstone, the famous African missionary and explorer. None of you ever saw James Watt, or Sir Walter Scott, or Robert Burns, or David Livingstone; but in George Square you may see their images, carved in marble or moulded in bronze; and these images give you some idea of what the men themselves were like.

Sometimes when a little boy is playing on the road, one person who is passing says to another, "Whose little boy is that?" And when he is told whose boy it is, he says, "Ah! I thought so. He's the very image of his father." So you see there are different kinds of images. A photograph in an album may be an image; a statue carved in stone may be an image; but the best image of all is the living image, the image that can run and think and speak.

Now God is a spirit. "No man hath seen God at any time." No man ever *could* see God. Where, then, shall we find an image of the invisible God?

Well, sometimes men have tried to make an image of God by carving a figure in wood or stone. In the temples of Greece long ago there were beautiful statues in marble, by the greatest sculptors that ever lived; and these statues were meant to be images of the invisible God. And in the heathen temples of India and China at the present day, there are ugly images—idols we call them; but the poor people who worship them think they are images of the invisible God. Some years ago I was in Rome, and I went to the Vatican Palace where the Pope lives, and saw the paintings in the famous picture - galleries. In some of the old paintings you may see a majestic figure that is meant to be an image of God. Great painters have painted these pictures, some of them probably the greatest painters the world has ever seen. But though the majestic figures are very grand as works of art, they are very poor as images of God.

No human eye has ever seen God's

face, and no human hand can make an image of the unseen God. But the text tells us that Jesus Christ is "the Image of the invisible God"; and in another place we read that He is "the brightness of the Father's glory, and the express Image of His Person." Just as a living boy with a mind that thinks, and a heart that loves, and lips that speak, and eyes that shine, is a much nobler and truer image of his father than any picture or statue can possibly be, so the best Image of God, the only true Image, is God's own Son, the Lord Jesus Christ. One of the disciples said to Jesus once, "Lord, show us the Father." Jesus answered, "He that hath seen Me hath seen the Father." In Jesus we see the perfect Image of God. And so if we want to know what God is like, and to have right thoughts about Him, we have just got to keep looking at Jesus. Sometimes, I believe, boys and girls are afraid of God, because they think of Him as a great and awful Being who lives far away in the sky. But you should think of God as He is revealed in Jesus Christ. All that Jesus is, God is. Remember, then, how gentle Jesus was, how fond of little children, how kind to the sorrowful, how willing to forgive sinners; and as you think of these things, you will understand what God is like. And if you always look at God in the face of Jesus Christ, and look at Jesus Christ as the true " Image of the invisible God," you will not be afraid of the heavenly Father, but will come to love Him more and more.

Lighthouses.

---*---

"Let your light so shine before men."—MATT.
v. 16.

IN the days when Jesus lived in
Palestine lighthouses were not very
common, and as Jesus did not live
near the coast of the open sea, it is quite
possible that He never saw one. And
yet, I think, we cannot get a better
illustration of the duty of letting our
light shine before men, than by watching
the light of the lighthouse as it shines
across the sea.

Many of you are accustomed to spend

your holidays at the seaside, and have often seen the well-known lighthouses of the Clyde—the Cloch, and Toward, and Cumbrae, and Pladda. It is a pleasant thing, when the darkness is coming on, to watch for the shining of the light, and to see it at last beaming brightly over the water. But if it is a pleasant sight to children at the seaside on a holiday, how much more welcome it is to the ships and steamers out at sea, especially if they are coming up the firth on a dark and cloudy night when the wind is blowing hard. Many a good ship would be lost, many a brave sailor would be drowned, if it were not for the shining of these lights.

Now Jesus wants you boys and girls to be like lighthouses shining on the sea. Let me suppose that you *are* little lighthouses, every one of you, and let me ask you three questions about your light.

1. *Why should you shine?*

The great reason is because the world is so dark. The ships do not need the light in the daytime, but when darkness comes on they need it very much. And the dark world is in great need of Christian light. Ignorance, and sorrow, and sin all combine to deepen the world's darkness; and therefore the children of Jesus must let their light shine, so as to warn men of their dangers, and to cheer them in their troubles, and to point them on their way. Will you seek to be *shining* lights? Will you think of the ignorant and the sorrowful, the tempted and the sinful, and try to guide them past the place of trials and dangers, and show them the way to Jesus Christ, the true harbour and refuge of the soul?

2. *How should you shine?*

You should shine brightly and steadily. Some dreadful shipwrecks have taken place of late years on the coast of Spain,

H

and our sailors and shipowners have complained that the Spanish lighthouses are not properly kept, for their lamps do not burn with a clear and steady radiance, like the lights on our British coasts. If a lighthouse does not shine with a bright and steady light, it may do more harm than good. And so the lighthouse keepers must be very particular about the quality of the light.

When I was a student I was sent for some weeks to preach among the Orkney Islands, and in one place the precentor in the church, who was a boatman, invited me to go with him to see a lighthouse. Every week he had to visit this lighthouse with provisions for the people who lived there. So we sailed away from the island of Stronsay to a lonely rock, or skerry as it is called, some miles from land, on which this lighthouse stands. The keeper showed me all that was to be seen ; and I can tell you that everything was done in that lighthouse to make the light burn bright and clear. The great reflectors were kept shining like mirrors, and the glasses of the cage were quite spotless and transparent, so that none of the light might be lost, but all of it might shine freely out across the sea.

Well, your light should shine like that. Don't allow any little faults and bad habits to gather like dirt on the windows of your soul. Don't shine on Sabbaths and grow dark on Mondays. Don't be well behaved in the church and ill behaved in the house or at the school. Seek to shine out always brightly and steadily, as children of Jesus, and "children of light."

3. My last question is this:—*Who is your lighthouse keeper?*

Every lighthouse needs a keeper, or the light would never shine. The keeper must supply the oil, and trim the wicks, and light the lamps. And if you boys and girls are to be little lighthouses in this dark world, you too must have a lighthouse keeper. Who then is your keeper? It must be Jesus. You cannot shine unless He brings the light into your heart, and gives you the oil that keeps the light from going out. And so if you wish to be lights in the world, you must come to Jesus day by day saying— " Lord, be Thou my keeper. Keep my heart, lest my light should go out. Help me to shine for Thee. And grant, when men see me shining, that they may be guided to the true haven, and may glorify my Father which is in heaven."

The Treasures of the Snow.

"Hast thou entered into the treasures (R.V. treasuries) of the snow?"—JOB xxxviii. 22.

YOU have come to church this morning through a world that is all white with snow; and I do not think that I could get a better subject than the snow about which to speak to you to-day. I am sure you were all surprised yesterday morning, when you got up and looked out of the window, to see that the snow had been falling through the night. The ground was deeply covered with it, and the trees were heavily laden, and the world was as beautiful as fairyland. Those of you who are strong and healthy were glad that the snow had come on Saturday morning, because there was no school to go to, and so you expected to have a long day's fun, making snow-houses and snow-men, and having splendid snow-fights.

But now I want you to turn from these *pleasures* of the snow to think of some of its spiritual *treasures*. Everything in God's world has some good lesson to teach us. A great poet tells us that we may find—

> " Tongues in trees, books in the running brooks,
> Sermons in stones, and good in everything."

And that is just what the Bible says, only instead of "good in everything," it says "God in everything." It tells us that we may learn about God from the lilies of the field, from the birds of the air, from the trees and rivers and mountains, from the blue sky and the dark clouds and the shining stars. And the snow also, according to the Bible, brings us a message from God. Let me tell you of three things about God which are found in "the treasuries of the snow."

1. The snow speaks to us of *God's purity.*

It comes down out of the sky, and it says, "How pure is God who lives up there, and who makes the beautiful snow-flakes, and scatters them abroad upon the earth." There is nothing in all the world so white as snow. If newly washed clothes are hung out to dry when snow is on the ground, how yellow and dirty they look beside it. Now, that pureness of the snow is like the purity of God. God is pure because He never did anything wrong; and heaven is pure because it is God's home. Nothing that defileth can enter there. And Jesus is pure because He is God's Son—the "Lamb without blemish and without spot." And God wants us to be pure also, so that we may come and live with Him. "Blessed are the pure in heart, for they shall see God." But how are we, with our sinful hearts, to get God's holy purity? Well, God Himself can make us pure. You have seen how the dirty muddy streets and the black ploughed fields become perfectly pure and white when God sends down the snow from heaven. And God who makes the black earth white, can make our black hearts white and pure.

We read in the book of *Revelation* of a great multitude before God's throne, "clothed with white robes, and palms in their hands." And how was that multitude all clothed in white? It was because they had "washed their robes, and made them white in the blood of the Lamb." Jesus can give us clean hearts, and clothe us in His own pure robe of righteousness. Would you like to have a clean heart and a pure snow-white robe? Then you must learn to pray this beautiful prayer, which a little boy of my acquaintance calls his "Snow Prayer," "Wash me, and I shall be whiter than snow!"

2. But the snow speaks to us not only of God's purity, but of *God's power.*

Did the snow ever make you think how great and powerful God must be? How is the snow made? God makes it out of the salt waves of the sea. His winds and sunbeams lift millions of tons of water high up into the air. This water, in the shape of clouds, is carried for hundreds of miles over sea and land. At length God changes the innumerable particles of water into beautiful snowflakes, and then down comes the snow, falling, falling, until the whole land is covered with it. And how awful is the power of God's snow! Gentle as a feather, and yet mightier than all the might of man. In some countries there are great glaciers and avalanches, that speak with a loud voice of the tremendous power of the snow.   But even in our own land we sometimes get proofs of its wonderful power.   It falls heavily for one night, and next day the streets are blocked up, the horses cannot go along the roads, even the great railway trains are perfectly helpless.   And if that happens when snow falls for a single night, just imagine what would happen if God made it fall for a whole week without ever ceasing.   The earth would be buried as under an avalanche, and people would die for want of fire and food.   How easily, you see, God could destroy the earth by snow, as He once destroyed it by water.   And so the little snowflakes speak to us of God's almighty power.

3. Once more the snow speaks to us of *God's promise.*

There is a passage in the Bible where a great prophet puts this beautiful saying into the mouth of God: "As the rain cometh down and the snow from heaven, and returneth not thither, but watereth the earth and maketh it bring forth and bud, that it may give seed to the sower and bread to the eater ; so shall My word be that goeth forth out of My mouth." You see what that means. Just as surely as the snow from heaven does not fall uselessly down, but helps the earth to bring forth its flowers and fruit, so surely shall the snowflakes of God's promise be followed in due season by the flowers and fruit of plentiful fulfilment.

And thus the snow becomes a beautiful sign to us that God's word of promise is sure. How full the Bible is of beautiful and precious promises, promises for the young and old, promises for this world and the next. Now, these promises can never fail ; that is one of the secrets which are whispered by the snow. But as the snow comes down to make the earth bring forth and bud, so shall the word be that our God hath spoken.

The Form of a Servant.

————✳————

"Christ Jesus, who . . . took upon Him the form of a servant."—PHIL. ii. 5-7.

DOESN'T it seem strange to think that Jesus Christ was a servant? He was the greatest and best man that ever lived. He was not only the best of men, but the very Son of God, the King of kings, and Lord of lords. And yet He "took upon Him the form of a servant." You remember something that Jesus did the very night before He died. He rose from the supper table, and took a towel, and tied it round His waist; then He poured some water into a basin, and began to wash His disciples' feet. Peter was ashamed to see Jesus doing such lowly work, and tried at first to prevent him. " Thou shalt never wash *my* feet!" he said. And we also are apt to feel, as Peter felt, that Jesus is too great and too good to do the work of a humble servant. But what Jesus did that night was only a symbol of what He did all through His life on earth. " He came not to be ministered unto, but to minister," *i.e.*, He came not to be served, but to be a servant. He never thought of His own comfort or pleasure, but spent all His time in serving others, and trying to make them both good and happy. He fed the hungry, and cured the sick, and comforted the sad, and forgave the sinful. And by all this Jesus has taught the world a new way of looking at service. It is no degradation to be a servant. It is the highest of all honours. "Whosoever will be chief among you," Jesus said, "let him be your servant."

If you should ever go to London, you will be sure to visit Westminster Abbey. There you will see the monuments of the Kings and Queens of England, and of many great men who have distinguished themselves in the history of our country. And among the others you will see a beautiful statue of white marble, with a very short inscription upon it—just these two words, "*Love! Serve!*"

That statue is the statue of Lord Shaftesbury. He was the son of an earl, and the heir to a great estate. Many a young man in his position would have lived a life of selfish pleasure, and would never have troubled himself about the sorrow and suffering that lie all around us. But when he was only a boy, little Lord Ashley (for that was his name before he succeeded his father as Earl of

Shaftesbury) gave his heart to Jesus Christ, through the faithful teaching of his nurse, Maria Millis; and very early in life he heard the voice of Jesus calling him to be a humble and devoted servant of his fellows. He was a pupil at Harrow School. And one day, as he was standing at the foot of Harrow Hill, a pauper's funeral passed along the road. There were no mourners at that funeral. The coffin was nothing but some rough boards loosely nailed together. The men who were driving it along in a cart were laughing and joking all the while. No one cared for this wretched pauper, and so his body was driven to the grave as if he were only a dead dog. In the ears of the sensitive boy who stood and watched this ghastly funeral, the jolting cart wheels were saying something like this :—

> "Rattle his bones
> Over the stones ;
> He's only a pauper
> Whom nobody owns."

Young Ashley was so shocked and pained by what he saw that day, that he made a vow to God, then and there, that he would give up his whole life to the service of the poor and the suffering. Not long since I was reading his life, and it was wonderful to see how nobly and completely his vow was fulfilled, until the name of Lord Shaftesbury became familiar throughout the length and breadth of the land, as the willing and loving servant of those who most needed to be pitied and helped. He spent his days and nights, both in and out of Parliament, in anxious toil for the boys and girls who worked in the factories, for the little chimney-sweeps who in those days had to climb up the narrow, dark, and dangerous chimneys, for the women who toiled like slaves or beasts of burden in the deep coal mines, and especially for the ragged children who ran about the city streets. On the morning after his death, a gentleman was walking along a street in London, when he passed two very ragged boys who were staring into a shop window; and as he passed he heard this conversation. The one said to the other, "Lord Shaftesbury's dead." "That's not *our* Lord Shaftesbury?" asked his companion. "Yes," replied the first, "it's *our* Lord Shaftesbury." The very city arabs, you see, knew that he loved them, and that he wished to be their ser ant and friend.

"*Love! Serve!*" Is not that a splendid epitaph to have upon one's tomb? Wouldn't you like to deserve that words like these should be applied to you? Then you must do as young Lord Ashley did. You must first take Jesus into your hearts, and then try to walk in His blessed footsteps. Will you not try this plan? Let love be your daily motive, and service your daily aim.

I

"Let this mind be in you which was also in Christ Jesus, who . . . made Himself of no reputation, and took upon Him the form of a servant."

The Peace=makers.

"Blessed are the peace-makers ; for they shall be called the children of God."—MATT. v. 9.

THERE are three great classes, I think, into which people might be divided—the peace-breakers, the peace-keepers, and the peace-makers.

1. First there are the *peace-breakers.*

Sometimes in the newspapers you will see that a man has been taken up by the police, and brought before the magistrates, for a breach of the peace ; and that just means for being a peace-breaker. He has been fighting on the street, or he has made such a noise, and gathered such a crowd, that the police have had to arrest him. But there are other ways of breaking the peace with which the police do not interfere, and which never get into the newspapers; and it is these other ways of which I am thinking at present. Here are two ladies who are very good friends; Mrs A. and Mrs B., we shall call them. But another lady, called Mrs C., says something to Mrs A. about Mrs B.; and then she says something to Mrs B. about Mrs A.; and after that the two old friends will hardly speak to each other any more. And the reason of it all is this, that Mrs C. is one of the peace-breakers.

Little girls sometimes begin to be peace-breakers at a very early age. There were two girls called Jeanie and Mary, who went to the same school, and played out on the road together on the summer evenings. But one day a little misunderstanding arose between them. It was not a thing of much importance, and they would soon have forgotten it and been fast friends again. But some other girls who knew about it, told Jeanie that Mary was "a horrid thing"; and they also told Mary that if they were in her shoes they would never speak to Jeanie again. And so the little tiff grew into a great quarrel, and all because there were some girls who chose to be peace-breakers.

And there are peace-breakers among the boys also. You may have seen a ring of boys standing on the road, with two little fellows in the middle. The two little boys were both looking rather frightened, as if they would have liked very much to run away to their mothers. Certainly neither of them was very anxious to fight. But the boys on one side said, "Hit him, Willie!" and the boys on the other side said, "Hit him, Johnnie!" and

by-and-by the two little fellows went
home to their mothers with bloody noses,
all because some other boys were among
the peace-breakers.

Now, boys and girls, don't be peace-
breakers whatever you are. Of all
wretched and contemptible persons, the
peace-breaker is amongst the worst. If
the peace-makers shall be called the
children of God, must we not say of the
peace-breakers that they are the children
of the devil? Sometimes I think that
the people who are taken up by the
police and brought before the magistrates
for disturbing the peace, are not nearly
so worthy to be put in jail as other peace-
breakers who escape without punishment,
although they have broken up old friend-
ships, and planted roots of bitterness in
loving hearts, and ruined the happiness
of many peaceful homes.

2. But pass now to the second class—
the *peace-keepers.*

These are people who do not like quarrelling and fighting. They prefer always to be at peace. It gives them no pleasure to see other people unhappy. And how pleasant it is, in a world that is full of strife and noise, to meet with people who love to be peaceful and kind. Remember, boys and girls, that it takes two to make a quarrel. If you try, as far as in you lies, to be lovers and keepers of peace, you will save both yourselves and others from a great deal of wretchedness and pain.

3. But there is something still better than being a peace-keeper, and that is to be a *peace-maker*.

Even people who love to keep peace are not always willing to make peace. It is not easy, when two of your friends have quarrelled, to go in between them and try to make them friendly again. If you do so, both of them are apt to be offended, and to think that you are favouring the opposite side. It is much easier to pretend to be on both sides, and not to interpose at all ; or else to keep as far as you can from both sides, saying to yourself, I don't want to get into hot water, I want to be at peace, and not to be mixed up with these miserable quarrels. But that is not the way which one of the true peace-makers will follow. He will run the risk of trouble to himself for the sake of healing a misunderstanding. He knows that neither party is quite so bad as the other thinks, and therefore he will try to make each side see how much can be said for the other side, how simply the misunderstanding arose, how easily it might have been explained at the first, and how much less black their neighbours are than their fancies have painted.

And now, boys and girls, I hope that you will seek to be peace-makers rather than peace-breakers. If you see others quarrelling, don't try to put coals on the fire, but rather to pour on some cold water. Remember these beautiful words of the Lord Jesus, " Blessed arc the peace-makers ; for they shall be called the children of God."

Entertaining Angels Unawares.

"Be not forgetful to entertain strangers; for thereby some have entertained angels unawares."
—HEB. xiii. 2.

THOSE of you who have Bibles with margins, will see a note in the margin opposite this verse, referring you to the chapter in Genesis which tells how Abraham one day entertained three strangers with hospitable kindness, and discovered by-and-by that he had been entertaining angels unawares. Perhaps you think that it is not likely that you will ever see angels coming to your door. And if by angels you mean such angels as Abraham saw, or such angels as you have seen in your picture-books, with white wings and shining garments, I think myself it is not likely that in this world you ever shall. It may be that millions of spiritual creatures walk the earth both when we wake and when we sleep, and that the angels of God are ever ascending and descending, as Jacob saw them in his vision, on that ladder of light. But just because the angels are spiritual creatures, we cannot see them with our eyes of flesh. They would need to come to us in a human form, as they came to Abraham, or our eyes would need to be opened as Jacob's eyes were opened whilst he slept, if we were to see the angels of heaven. But God has other angels besides the angels who are invisible. These angels often come knocking at our door. And we never know, when we are entertaining a stranger, but we may be entertaining an angel unawares.

Let me tell you a beautiful story which is told in one of the books of a great English writer. I hope that by-and-by you will read the story for yourselves. There was once a poor weaver who lived not far from a quiet old-fashioned village. He had had great trials in his earlier years, and had been treated very unjustly and cruelly by other people. This had led him to shut himself up in his cottage, and never speak to his neighbours if he could possibly help it. The only thing he cared for was the money he earned by his loom. All the money he got he changed into sovereigns, and he kept the sovereigns in a bag hidden in a hole under one of the stone flags of his kitchen floor. And every night when his work was done he lifted the stone, and took out his bag, and let the gold run through his fingers, and counted it over and over again. Oh! how he loved those sovereigns! But there was nothing else in the world that he loved. He was very hard and cold and selfish; for he had shut the door of his heart against all his fellow-creatures.

One night when he was out, a thief came in and stole the bag with all the money he had been gathering for so many years. When the poor weaver came back and found that his gold was gone, the shock of his grief almost drove him mad. Day after day he sat by the fire quite dazed and stupid. But one evening when he had been sitting for a while half unconscious, he noticed as he awoke from his stupor that something just like yellow gold was glancing and shining on the floor in the ruddy light of the fire. He was very short-sighted, and for a moment he thought that his

money had come back. So he sprang
forward, and clutched at it with eager
fingers. But what do you think he
found? A little girl with golden hair
lying on the floor fast asleep. Her
mother was a poor woman who had
perished that night in the snow quite
near to the weaver's door; and the little
girl, seeing the light of the fire shining
through the window, had wandered in
and lain down in the warm room to sleep.
Well, there was no one to claim this
little orphan, and so the weaver kept her
himself. And soon he came to love her
far more than he had ever loved his gold;
and through her, after a while, he learned
to love his neighbours also. So she became his ministering angel, turning his
hard and selfish heart to thoughts of
gentleness and kindness. Her little hand
was put in his "to lead him forth gently
towards a calm and bright land."

Now, I shall tell you another story;

for I believe that you children like stories best of all.

There was once a little orphan boy in Germany, who lived in a home for poor children founded by John Falk, a very good man, somewhat like our Mr Quarrier, who did a great deal for the poor orphans. It was supper time. One of the bigger boys was told to ask the blessing, and he repeated the words which were used in the home at meal time every night, "Come, Lord Jesus, be our guest, and bless what Thou hast provided." And then the little boy looked up and said, "But why does Jesus never come? We ask Him every night to come and sit with us, and He never comes." The teacher said, "Oh yes! my child, only believe that Jesus will come, and you may be sure He *will* come, for He does not despise our invitation." "Then," said the little boy, "if He is coming, I will put in this chair for Him." Just with that there was a knock at the door, and a poor shivering boy came in and begged for a night's shelter. He was made welcome, and the teacher told him to sit in the empty chair. And then the little boy, who had been thinking very hard all the time, said, "Perhaps Jesus could not come to-night, and so He sent this poor boy instead."

Don't you think that little boy was right? If we are kind to the poor and the strangers, we are entertaining, not angels only, but Jesus Christ, the Lord of all the angels. For Jesus has said, "Inasmuch as ye have done it unto one of the least of these My brethren, ye have done it unto Me."

Will you boys and girls try to be kind to the strangers and the poor? Sometimes when a new boy comes to school, the other boys worry him just because he is a stranger. And sometimes when a girl is poorer than the rest, the other girls treat her in a way which makes her miserable.

But remember what Jesus says about being kind to His poor friends, and remember also the words of this beautiful text, "Be not forgetful to entertain strangers; for thereby some have entertained angels unawares."

Contentment.

"Be content with such things as ye have."—
HEB. xiii. 5.

CONTENTMENT is a grace which is often spoken about in the Bible, and it is a grace which greatly needs to be spoken about still. There are multitudes of people who possess many of the other Christian graces, but cannot be said to "abound in this grace also." How common it is to meet with men and women who are always discontented, and always grumbling. Indeed, I'm afraid that in

the world there are even a great many
discontented boys and girls. They are
discontented with their food, or with
their clothes, or with their toys; or they
are discontented with things in general,
they cannot tell you what or why.

Did you ever hear the story of the
discontented fish and the discontented
canary? They lived in the same
parlour. The fish had a nice large
globe full of water to swim in, and the
canary was hung up in the window in
a beautiful cage. One hot summer day
they both began to grumble. The fish
said: "I wish I could sing like that
canary. I wish I lived up yonder in
that beautiful cage." And the canary,
who was feeling very warm, said: "Oh
how I wish that I lived down there in
that cool globe of water where the fish
is swimming to and fro." Suddenly a
voice said: "Canary, go down to the
water. Fish, go up to the cage." Im-

mediately they exchanged places. And how happy they were then! How delighted the fish was with the cage! How comfortable the canary felt in the water! I see you are smiling at the fish and the canary; but, after all, they are just like some people who are never content with what they have, and would like to change places with somebody else; although, if they did, they would certainly be much more miserable than they were before.

I might give you many reasons for seeking to have contentment. Let me mention only two.

One is because *contentment will make you beautiful.* That is a reason especially for the girls. You would like to be beautiful, I am sure. Well, Christian contentment is one great secret of beauty. There is a kind of beauty which soon fades away; it is only skin-deep. But there is another kind of

beauty which lasts. I read in a paper
lately that a lady who is one of the
most famous singers in the world, and
who always looks both fresh and youth-
ful, although she is no longer young,
was asked how it is that her face seems
never to grow old. "I cannot tell," she
said, "unless it is because I have made
it a rule of my life *never* to be cross
and *never* to be discontented." Now, I
cannot promise you that contentment
will keep *your* faces from growing old;
but I am sure of this that it will keep
them from ever growing ugly. No
person with a contented heart ever had
an ugly face. The older such persons
grow, their faces only get the more
beautiful, as all the pleasant thoughts
and kindly feelings in their hearts get
written down upon their features.

But another reason why you should
be contented is, because *contentment will
make you happy.* Nothing in the world

can make discontented people happy. All kinds of gifts and blessings may be showered upon them; but they persist in thinking not of what they have, but of what they have not. They are like the boy I have read of who only wanted a knife, but when he got the knife he only wanted a ball, and when he got the ball he only wanted a top, and when he got the top he only wanted a kite; and when he had knife and ball and top and kite, still he was not happy, because he was not contented. To try to be happy without contentment is like trying to carry water in a sieve. You may dip the sieve into the water, but the water all runs through the holes. While a heart that is contented cannot help being happy. It has no holes for the water to run through. It keeps all it gets, and so it is full of joy.

But how are we to get contentment?

Well, here is one way. We must look on the bright side of things. It's not what we have, so much as our way of looking at it, that makes us contented or discontented. Two pitchers were once going to the well. Said the one to the other, "How black and dismal you seem to be this morning." "Ah!" the other pitcher replied, "I was just thinking how useless it is to come to the well day after day, for however full we go away, we always come back empty." "Dear me!" said the first pitcher, "how strange to look at it in that way. Now, I was just thinking how good it is that though we come here perfectly empty, we always go away again filled up to the brim."

That's the way to be contented. There's a bright side and a dark side to everything. Look on the bright side. Don't keep saying to yourself, How selfish people are; how unkind everybody is; how many troubles I have to bear. Think rather,

How good God is; how loving is Jesus who came from the sky; how many kind friends I have; how many comforts and blessings. And then, like the contented pitcher, your heart will always sing for joy.

The Rock that is Higher.

"Lead me to the Rock that is higher than I."—
Ps. lxi. 2.

THE Psalm from which these words
are taken was written by David,
the shepherd boy who became a
king. For a long part of his life David
was an outlaw. King Saul had put a
price upon his head, and cruel men were
hunting for him everywhere throughout
the land. Some of you have read about
the Covenanters, Peden the Prophet, and
Donald Cargill, and James Renwick, and

Richard Cameron, and Captain Paton of
Meadowhead whose Bible and sword may
still be seen at Lochgoin farmhouse. You
know how those men were hunted on
the moors and mountains, and how to
this day the country people in Ayrshire
and Dumfriesshire will show you the
caves in which some of them are said to
have hid.

Well, David had to flee to the mountains; but the mountains were not like
most of our Scottish mountains. They
were not beautiful slopes and heights
covered with grass and heather, but an
awful wilderness of bare jagged rocks—
not a beautiful sight to look at, nor a
comfortable place to live in. But David
loved these rocks, because they had been
his hiding-place, and had saved him
from the cruel hands of his enemies.
And because David loved the rocks
so much, he came to think that God
was like a rock. Again and again, I

don't know how often, we find him in his Psalms calling God a rock. " The Lord is my Rock," he says. " The Lord liveth, and blessed be my Rock." " He only is my Rock and my salvation." And when he says in this verse, " Lead me to the Rock that is higher than I," he means, by that Rock which is higher, no other than God Himself.

Let me tell you of three reasons that David had for calling God his Rock :—

1. In the first place God was *a Rock of Refuge.*

Sometimes when David awoke in the morning, he saw far away down in the valley the glint of the morning sun on the spears of a body of soldiers ; and he knew that those men were going to hunt for him all day long, and try to capture, or to kill him. If David had been in a wide plain, he would have had little chance of escape ; he must soon have been seen and caught. But the rocks were his refuge. He climbed higher and higher, until he came to some dark cave known only to himself, and there he found a refuge until the danger was past.

Now God is a Rock of Refuge to every one who trusts in Him. If we are in danger or trouble, we can always go to God, and He will help us. When our hearts are overwhelmed and in perplexity, we can cry, as David did, " Lead me to the Rock that is higher than I." And then we shall find, as David found, that God is our Rock and our salvation, and our "very present help in trouble."

2. But, again, God was not only a Rock of Refuge from the enemy, but *a Rock of Shadow from the heat.*

We can hardly understand in our temperate climate the heat from which men sometimes suffer in a land like Palestine— the sun blazing like a ball of fire, not a cloud in the sky to screen its scorching rays, not a breath of air to temper them ; until at length strong men feel as if they would faint away, or even fall down and die. How pleasant it must be in such a land, when one is walking through a wilderness of sand, or climbing up a mountain side, to come to a great high rock that stands straight up and casts a deep cool shadow. David had often felt the delight which comes from " the shadow of a great rock in a weary land "; and so he came to think of God as a shelter and shadow from the heat. Is it not a beautiful thought, that God is not only our refuge from special dangers, but also our refreshing shadow from the burden and the heat of every common day? Sometimes our hearts get very hot and flustered amidst all our daily tasks and toils. Let us go then in thought and in prayer to the Rock that is higher than we, so that coolness and calm and peace may come back to our souls.

3. Once more David thought of God
as the "*Rock of Ages.*"

Nothing gives us such an impression of
unchanging strength as a great mountain
peak. Some of you have been in Arran
for your holidays, and most of you have
seen the Arran hills from the Ayrshire
coast, or from one of the Clyde steamers.
Well, the peak of Goatfell is practically
the same as it was nearly six hundred
years ago, when King Robert the Bruce
stayed in Arran, and watched and waited
every night to see that beacon on the
Carrick shore, of which you have read in
your "History of Scotland." A mountain
is a symbol of strength that does not
change ; and so a mountain rock is a
symbol of God. His righteousness, and
His love also, are "like the great mountains." He is "the same yesterday, to-
day, and for ever." He is the "Rock of
Ages." David had found that men are
always changing. Some of his friends

grew false, and deserted him. King Saul first showed him great favour, and then tried to take away his life. His beloved Jonathan always remained faithful and true; but death came and took Jonathan away. But God was a strong Rock, a Rock that could not be shaken, a Rock to which David could continually resort when his heart was overwhelmed. Will you not put your trust, dear children, in the everlasting God, and in Jesus Christ His Son, our Saviour, that "Rock of Ages" of whom we have been singing, whose side was riven for our sakes, so that we might find a hiding-place in the "clefts of the Rock"?

The Kingdom of God.

"Fear not, little flock ; for it is your Father's good pleasure to give you the kingdom." — LUKE xii. 32.

WHAT a wonderful gift is promised in this text—the gift of a kingdom! We read of some great conquerors who gave kingdoms to their friends, and Jesus says it is our Father's good pleasure to give *us* the kingdom.

I wonder where that kingdom is. Most of you are learning geography, and if we had a map of the world here, you would soon point out its states and kingdoms — Great Britain, and France, and Germany, and all the rest. But you would not find the kingdom of which I am speaking on any map of the world. This kingdom is the kingdom of God, and no geographer has mapped it out. You cannot point to it in an atlas and say, "Lo! it is here," or "Lo! it is there."

Where, then, is the kingdom of God? Perhaps some one says it is up in heaven, for Jesus often called it "the kingdom of heaven." But where is heaven? Up in the sky, you answer, far above the stars, where Jesus dwells with the saints and angels. Yes, the kingdom of heaven *is* there; but it is also here in this world in which we live.

Do you little boys ever play at trains? My little boy often does. A "puff-puff," as he calls it, has a wonderful fascination for him, as it has for most boys. Well, a little boy and his younger

L

sister were "playing train" one day. He was the engine, and she was all the passengers rolled into one. He was determined to get a big enough place to start from, and so he shouted "London," and then went puffing, puffing, all round the room. In a little while he stopped and called out, "Edinburgh," and then again he stopped and called out, "Glasgow!" But the next time he stopped, his geography was quite exhausted, and so, as he didn't remember any other place, he shouted, "Heaven!" Now, that little boy was not thinking what he said when he shouted "Heaven!"; and yet, perhaps, he was not very far wrong, for the kingdom of heaven is here in the world as well as up above the sky. The kingdom of heaven is in London, and in Edinburgh, and in Glasgow, and also here in Cathcart. For wherever there are men and women, or boys and girls, who love the Lord Jesus, God's kingdom of heaven is there. "The kingdom of God," said Jesus, "is within you,"—inside of your heart.

And is not this the best kind of kingdom? Earthly kingdoms may be taken away, but this is "a kingdom which cannot be moved." And again, earthly kingdoms bring with them a great deal of trouble and sorrow and care. "Uneasy lies the head that wears a crown." But happy are they who have got the gift of the Father's kingdom, for this kingdom, Paul tells us, "is righteousness and peace and joy in the Holy Ghost."

But how are you to get this wonderful gift of the kingdom of God? Just by taking Jesus Christ into your heart. Let him in, and He will put the Father's crown upon your head. Some of you have admitted Jesus already. You are kings and queens in the kingdom of your Father. But Jesus wants you all to be kings and queens. Won't you ask the

Saviour in, so that you may receive the
Father's gift? Won't you say, in the
words of the beautiful children's hymn
we sometimes sing :—

> "Oh, come to my heart, Lord Jesus,
>   There is room in my heart for Thee ! "

And now read the text over again: "Fear
not, little flock ; for it is your Father's
good pleasure to give you the kingdom."
Why did Jesus say, "Fear not, little flock?"
His disciples were troubling themselves
about many things—about food, and clothing, and other worldly cares. But Jesus
said, Why trouble yourself about such
things, when it is your Father's good
pleasure to give you *the kingdom ?* If
God makes you kings and queens, He will
surely give you food and clothing. If He
gives you His own Son, how shall He
not with Him also freely give you all
things ?

The children of God should never be
afraid. Much less should they be filled

with fear concerning little things. The love which gives the greater blessing will certainly supply the less. The Father who gives us the kingdom, may be trusted to give us "all good things."

Burden=Bearing.

"Bear ye one another's burdens, and so fulfil the law of Christ."—GAL. vi. 2.

WHEN the apostle tells us to bear one another's burdens, he evidently takes for granted that we all have burdens to bear. And so, undoubtedly, we have. Did you ever see a regiment of soldiers in full marching dress, every one with his knapsack on his back? They are just like the men and women and boys and girls who are marching on the journey of life. We don't carry our burdens in knapsacks. Perhaps no one sees the burdens that we bear. But every one of us has a burden. And, more than that, every one must carry his burden for himself. You can't carry my burden, and I can't carry yours. The apostle says in the fifth verse of this same chapter, "Every man shall bear his own burden."

If you have lessons to learn, no one else can learn them for you. If I came and learned them all by heart, it would do you no good. You would be no better off than you were before. You would still have to learn them for yourselves.

If you have suffering to bear, no one else can bear it for you. Sometimes when a mother sees her little child in suffering she wishes, oh how much! that she could bear the pain and let the little one escape. But she cannot do it. The child must bear its own burden.

And, again, if you have done something wrong, you cannot lay the re-

sponsibility upon other shoulders. Sometimes children try to do that. They say,
"It was not my fault!" They wish to
put all the blame on somebody else,—a
brother or a sister or a playmate, just as
Adam wanted to put the blame on Eve,
and Eve wanted to put the blame on
Satan. But if you have done wrong, it
is *you* that have done it; and *you* must
bear the burden of responsibility to God.
Perhaps others have done wrong too. If
so, they have their own burden of blame.
But that does not free you from your
burden.

And, yet, although every one must bear
his own burden, the apostle says, "Bear
ye one another's burdens, and so fulfil
the law of Christ." Now, what does he
mean by that? How can we bear the
burdens of other people?

We can do it by *sympathy.* It is true
that every man must bear his own
burden, and yet by sympathy we can

make our neighbour's burden lighter, and help him to bear it more bravely and patiently and cheerfully than before.

Sometimes in the evening your father comes home from business worried and tired. If you choose you can make his burden heavier still, by being noisy and quarrelsome and disobedient. But instead of that you say to yourself: " Father looks tired to-night. I will try to be as good as possible, and to make the evening as pleasant as I can." And if you really try, you have no idea what a blessing you can be to your father, and how he often thanks God, when he is bearing the burden and heat of the day in the great city, that he has a bright and happy home to come to at night.

And has not your mother a burden also, with a whole household to look after? Is she not sometimes quite worn out with all her daily burden - bearing?

And couldn't you do a great deal, if you chose, to make her burden lighter by your sympathy and help?

Sometimes at school there is a scholar who has to bear a heavy burden. Perhaps it is a boy who is lame, and who cannot run about like other boys. Perhaps it is a girl who is poor, and who is not so nicely dressed as other girls. Some boys. and girls make the burden heavier for their less fortunate companions, by laughing at them, or avoiding them, or saying unkind things about them. Will you make up your minds to do to others as you would like them to do to you, and try to show special kindness to those who need your kindness most of all?

What a beautiful thing sympathy is! How it brightens the world to those who are sad and weary, falling on them like the sunlight of a bright morning, which makes our day's burden seem easier to bear. And what a hideous thing selfishness is! How it hardens the heart, until there is no place left for sympathy at all. Sydney Smith once said of a man he knew: "That man is so hard that you might drive a broad-wheeled waggon over him, and it would produce no impression. If you were to bore holes in him with a gimlet, I am convinced that sawdust would come out."

I am sure you would not like to become like that. Well, if you wish to be saved from becoming like that, you should begin when you are young to practise "the law of kindness." There is a society which is called "The Guild of Kindness." It is made up of young people who have pledged themselves to do a kind act, or speak a kind word, every day of their lives to some fellow-creature. Is it not a splendid idea? Would it not be a good thing for us all, even though we do not belong to

"The Guild of Kindness," to resolve to keep "the law of kindness" every day, so that we might make the lives of others brighter, and their burdens easier to bear?

"Bear ye one another's burdens, *and so fulfil the law of Christ.*" That is the great reason for doing it, because it is Christ's law, His golden rule. Will you ask God to give you more sympathy, so that you may be able to "fulfil the law of Christ"? Will you make these beautiful words of one of our beautiful hymns a part of your daily prayer:

"I ask Thee for a thoughtful love,
    Through constant watching wise;
    .   .   .   .   .
And a heart at leisure from itself,
    To soothe and sympathise"?

A
Scholar of Conscience.

———◆◦◆———

"But so did not I, because of the fear of God."
—NEH. v. 15.

IN the afternoons I often meet boys
and girls coming home from school
with their books in their hands,
and if I stop and speak to them, I find
that at the school they are learning a
great many different things from different lesson-books. One of their books is
a reading book, and another a geography,
and another an arithmetic; and the older
scholars have French and Latin books as

well. Those are the lessons you have to learn at school; and sometimes, I fancy, you are glad to think that by-and-by your schooldays will all be over, and you will have no more lessons to learn.

But there is another school in which the scholars are men and women as well as boys and girls. The scholars here can never lay their lesson-books aside; for the name of the school is the School of Life. And in this school there is a teacher about whom I wish to tell you. His name is Mr Conscience. And Mr Conscience has two favourite lesson-books, one of them called "Do!" and the other called "Don't!" from which, to the very end of our lives, we all have lessons to learn.

Nehemiah, the author of this book from which the text is taken, was a scholar in the school of Mr Conscience. And a very good scholar Nehemiah was. Mr Conscience had put into his hands the lesson-book called "DON'T!" He had taught him that there were some things which for God's sake he must not do; and Nehemiah is able to say: "So did not I, because of the fear of God."

Now, you boys and girls have to learn the same lesson as was learned by Nehemiah. Conscience tells you that there are some things which you must not do. Perhaps you would like very much to do them. But Conscience holds up his book before your eyes and says: "No! no! you must not do so, for God would be displeased."

There was something which made it specially noble for Nehemiah to keep from doing the things he speaks about, and that was that other men round about were doing those very things. It is not easy when every one about us is doing wrong to keep from doing it ourselves. It is always hard to stand alone. But if we would be true scholars of Mr

Conscience, that is what we shall often have to do. Other boys may do a thing, other girls may do it ; but if Conscience says "*Don't!*" we must stand bravely out like Nehemiah, who said, "So did not I, because of the fear of God."

Some of you have read that splendid book for boys, "Tom Brown's School-days." You remember that when Tom Brown went to Rugby the boys who slept in his dormitory never said their prayers. Some of them when they first came to the school, would have liked to kneel down and pray, as they had been accustomed to do at home; but no one else did it, and they were afraid to begin. But one day a new boy came to the school, a little fellow called Arthur, a pale-faced, delicate child. And that little boy had the courage to do what bigger and stronger boys had not done. He was not ashamed to show his colours. On his very first night at Rugby he knelt down beside his bed, and prayed to his heavenly Father. A big, brutal fellow in the middle of the room shied his slipper at the kneeling boy; but Tom Brown, as you know, took Arthur's part that night, and, more than that, Tom Brown knelt down himself next morning to pray to God, and by-and-by nearly all the boys in the room followed the lead which Arthur and Tom had given, and said their prayers every morning and every night.

One day some boys were playing with a ball near to a window, when somehow or other the ball went crashing through a pane. In a moment the boys made for the corner, and when the man whose window was broken got to the door they had all disappeared. No, not all. There was one boy who stayed behind. He would have liked, oh so much! to run away too. It was terribly hard to stay when he saw all the others vanishing

M

round the corner. But his conscience would not let him. It said, "To run away would be a mean and cowardly thing, and you must not be a coward." And so he bravely stayed behind, and gave his name, and promised that he would help to pay for the broken glass.

Now, boys, I want to ask you two questions. What would you have done if you had been one of those boys? Would you have run away, or would you have stayed behind? That's my first question. And my other question is this—What was the right thing to do? I don't know what your answer to the first question would be; but I am sure of this, that if you think about the matter for a single moment, you will feel that the brave thing and the right thing was —not to run away, but to stay and confess the truth.

God help you all to be good scholars in the school of Mr Conscience, not afraid to say NO! not afraid to stand alone; but taking as your motto the brave words of Nehemiah, "So did not I, because of the fear of God."

Christim our Master.

"Ye call Me Master (διδάσκαλος) and Lord: and
ye say well; for so I am."—JOHN xiii. 13.

"Master (ἐπιστάτα), we have toiled all the night."
—LUKE v. 5.

I F you search the New Testament to
find out the different names and
titles which are given to Jesus, you
will hardly find any, I think, which is
more often used than the name "Master."
I looked up my concordance, and I found
that more than sixty times Jesus is
called by this name. Some of you know
that the New Testament was written in
Greek, and that *our* New Testament is

only a translation. Well, when we turn
to the Greek Testament, we find that it
is not always the same word in the Greek
which has been translated into "Master"
in the English version. There is one
Greek word which means master in the
sense of teacher or schoolmaster. But
there is another which means master in
the sense of overseer or commander.
And as Jesus is called by both of these
names, we must think of Him both as
our Schoolmaster, and our Commander, if
we are to understand all that His title
of "Master" implies.

1. Jesus is our *Schoolmaster.*

When you go to school you first learn
to read, and then when you are older
you are taught writing and arithmetic
and history and geography and many
other things. But Jesus teaches you what
is better than reading or writing or arithmetic. He teaches you about God, and
He teaches you to be good. And that

is the best knowledge in all the world.
It is very nice to be clever, no doubt,
and to sit at the top of the class, and to
get prizes when the examination comes;
but to be true and honest, to be loving
and obedient, is better by far.

When you go to school, you mean to
go only for a few years. Soon your
childhood will pass away, and your
schooldays will be done. But Christ's
pupils are never done with their school-
ing. All through their lives their educa-
tion is going on. When you see an
old white-haired Christian sitting in the
church, you see an old disciple of Jesus
Christ, and a disciple just means a pupil.
Even old Christians have still much need
of the great Master's teaching. And even
in heaven we shall still have to go to
Christ's school; for we shall still have
many things to learn.

When boys and girls are at school,
they need to have school-books. And

school-books are needed also at the school
of Jesus.   Can you tell me, I wonder,
what some of Christ's school books are?
One is the beautiful world in which we
live.   Our Master gives us lessons from
the lilies of the field, and the birds of
the air, and the trees of the wood, and
the clouds of the skies.   All these have
messages to bring us, and if we listen to
Jesus He will tell us what their messages
are.   Another lesson-book is the lesson-
book of experience.   All our tasks and
toils, all our trials and temptations, all
our joys and sorrows, are lessons from
the book of experience.   Sometimes these
lessons are very hard ; but Jesus can
always tell us what every lesson means.
Another lesson-book is the Bible.   The
Bible is full of the most wonderful and
precious lessons, and so all pupils in the
school of Christ must seek to know their
Bibles.   You boys and girls should read
the Bible every day, you should store

up its golden texts in your hearts, you should think about their meaning, and listen attentively when your teachers in the Sabbath school are trying to make that meaning plain.

2. Jesus is our *Commander.*

We must think now of this other meaning of the word Master. When you boys go away from school and get into business, you have a different kind of master from the schoolmaster. In a warehouse, or an office, or a workshop, you have a master who commands you, whose servant you are, and whose orders you are bound to obey. And Jesus is our Master in this sense also ; for we are not only His pupils, but His servants.

When a boy leaves school and goes into business, he generally feels quite proud of his promotion. He feels that now at length he is going to be a man. He takes a great pride in the business with which he is connected, and when

he refers to it, talks about "our firm,"
and "our house," and "our shop." Some
of you, no doubt, are wearying to begin
business, and hoping to get into the
service of a good employer. Well, here
is a Master whose service you can enter
immediately. You don't need to wait
until your schooldays are done. There
are thousands of schoolboys and school-
girls who are engaged in Christ's service
already, and are trying every day, in
thought and word and deed, to do and
to be what will best please their Master.

Sometimes when a boy applies for a
situation, and goes to the office to see
the master, the master looks at him from
head to foot, and then says, "I'm afraid,
my boy, you are too young for this
place." But Jesus never says that to
anybody. "Suffer *little* children to come
unto Me," He says. "I want them all.
I have work in My kingdom for every
one of them to do." And so, if you are

willing to be Christ's servants, you have only got to apply for a place, and this great Master will take you at once into His employment, and show you how you may glorify His name.

SOME OPINIONS of the PRESS

ON THE

"GOLDEN NAILS" SERIES.

"The outstanding feature of the Addresses is their simplicity and suitability for the minds and wants of the little ones for whom they were printed. The language is simple, the addresses are short, and the lessons taught are illustrated by suitable stories, without which the attention of the young cannot readily be sustained."—*Dundee Advertiser.*

"Will delight those whose life is yet all before them ; and more, will aid, pleasantly and quietly and surely, in forming that groundwork of preparedness which goes so far to make life worth living."—*Liverpool Post.*

"Conveying lessons of wisdom, kindness, and humility so attractively, that boys and girls, and their elders too, will read with delight and profit."—*Pray and Trust.*

"Well planned, simple in language, pointed, and filled with apt and telling illustrations."—*North British Daily Mail.*

"Every volume has had a good reception, and every new volume increases one's admiration for the enterprise. We have always felt that if three things were made imperative—freshness, truth, and cheapness—there was a great field for children's sermons, for we knew that there were children and children's preachers who were hungering and thirsting after them as after righteousness itself. The latest volume of the 'Golden Nails' Series is as happy as its happy title. It is worthy of its place."—*Expository Times.*

"Written in a bright, easy, and popular style, and the sound, practical advice that they give is appropriately illustrated by a copious supply of anecdotes drawn from history. Children should read them with interest."—*Scotsman.*

"Models of brevity, clearness, and attractiveness."—*Kilmarnock Standard.*

"Characterised by simplicity of diction, suitable illustration, and commendable brevity." — *Hamilton Advertiser.*

"Should prove a boon to Sabbath School teachers."—*Hawick Advertiser.*

"A worthy addition to a list of bright and interesting addresses or sermonettes to children. The language is simple, and the illustrations being drawn from everyday life, bring the lessons easily within the grasp of quite young children."—*S.S. Chronicle.*

"Simple, practical, and pointed, neither a 'taking down' nor a 'strain up.'"—*Christian Leader.*

"The addresses are admirably suited to their audience. The style is simple, the divisions are felicitous, and the teachings are wholesome and practical." — *Glasgow Herald.*

"Containing twenty lovely addresses, in each of which a father's heart tenderly yearns over the children to whom he thus speaks. The stories, which form a pro-minent feature in the most successful of such sermons, are well chosen, and not by any means of an antiquated type, and parent, preacher, and teacher may read with pleasure and profit."—*Methodist Recorder.*

"These addresses can be heartily commended, for they are sure to exercise a healthy influence upon the minds of juvenile readers. Not only are the thoughts and senti-ments unexceptional, but they are clothed in graceful and impressive language."—*Dundee Courier.*

"The sermons are such as children can understand and value. The language is plain and direct, and not a few incidents related are new in the connections in which they are found. It is a wholesome book."—*Youth.*

"An admirable collection, which has done so much to popularise sermons and addresses specially intended for the young. The truths enforced are presented in a most attractive manner."—*Christian Commonwealth.*

Post 8vo, neat cloth, 1s. 6d.

Golden Nails,

And other Addresses to Children,

By the Rev. GEORGE MILLIGAN, B.D.

Sixth Thousand.

"The outstanding feature of the addresses is their simplicity and suitability for the minds and wants of the little ones for whom they were printed. The language is simple, the addresses are short, and the lessons taught are illustrated by suitable stories, without which the attention of the young cannot readily be sustained."—*Dundee Advertiser.*

"These are the work of a diligent man, who works as conscientiously at his preaching to children as at his most ambitious sermons. He plainly uses a commonplace book, or has a memory which he can use for the same purpose; and so on every possible subject he has store of anecdotes, familiar and unfamiliar, which he tells with a fine sincerity which could not fail to be impressive. The art of preaching to children has not been fully studied yet, and some great preachers have shown that incessant stories are not the only way to the child's heart; Dr Dods managed in his Glasgow days to put a deal of solid thinking into his addresses, which satisfied children just as much as their parents. But great preachers are rare, and Mr Milligan has given a most excellent collection of the commoner type of children's sermon, which will be welcomed in many homes and used by many hard-pressed preachers whose own stores of illustration are exhausted."—*Christian Leader.*

"Twenty attractive talks to the little ones."—*Christian.*

"A series of twenty excellent Sunday-School addresses. These addresses are like good nails, straight and pointed, full of illustrations, and such as children will delight to hear."—*Sunday-School Chronicle.*

"Every sermon has a message that children can understand, and the message is delivered in a way that children love. The preacher has a good stock of illustrations, and not by any means an ancient one. What Mr Milligan has preached is sure to be preached again, and not in vain."—*Methodist Times.*

EDINBURGH AND LONDON

OLIPHANT ANDERSON & FERRIER

And all Booksellers.

Post 8vo, Cloth Extra, Price 1s. 6d.

"Silver Wings."

And other Addresses to Children.

By the Rev. ANDREW G. FLEMING.

"An admirable volume of addresses to children—simple, practical, earnest, and above all abounding in appropriate illustration."—*New Age.*

"Well planned, simple in language, pointed, and filled with apt and telling illustrations. The book cannot fail to be a great favourite with the young."—*North British Daily Mail.*

"Every volume has had a good reception, and every new volume increases one's admiration for the enterprise. We have always felt that if three things were made imperative—freshness, truth, and cheapness—there was a great field for children's sermons, for we knew that there were children and children's preachers who were hungering and thirsting after them as after righteousness itself. The latest volume of the 'Golden Nails Series' is as happy as its happy title. It is worthy of its place."—*Expository Times.*

"A delightful, readable book, and most suitable for young folks."—*British Messenger.*

"Written in a bright, easy, and popular style, and the sound, practical advice that they give is appropriately illustrated by a copious supply of anecdotes drawn from history. Children should read them with interest."—*Scotsman.*

EDINBURGH AND LONDON

OLIPHANT, ANDERSON & FERRIER,

AND ALL BOOKSELLERS.

Post 8vo, neat cloth, price 1s. 6d.

Kingless Folk,

And other Addresses on Bible Animals.

By JOHN ADAMS, B.D.

"The information conveyed concerning common things makes the book instructive, the simplicity, yet beauty, of its style gives it attractiveness, and the method employed in arranging the parts of each proves the capacity of the writter for giving constructive proportion and plan to thought."—*Educational News.*

"The 'Kingless Folk' are ants, and the neat little volume contains eighteen addresses to children on Bible animals. Bees and bears, doves and coneys, eagles and oysters, lions and cocks, are among the creatures selected for notice. The fresh, bright style of the writer, the accuracy of his information, and the usefulness of the religious and moral lessons he draws from the birds and the other creatures he describes, will render his book a treasure to young people in the nursery or schoolroom." —*The Record.*

"The addresses are pithily written, the anecdotes are admirably chosen, and the style is very fascinating. They are models of conciseness, and combine practical information with healthy religious sentiment."—*People's Journal.*

"Charming addresses to young people on Bible animals."— *Kilmarnock Herald.*

"Just as pleasant as its predecessors, just as human and childlike, just as outward and attractive, just as evangelical and impressive, just as sure of complete success."—*Expository Times.*

"This is a delightful boy's book. It is bright all through, but is occasionally made brighter yet by a bit of genuine humour. Mr Adams takes his young friends out into the wide domain of nature, and interprets to them the lesson taught by ant and bee and bear, by the ass's colt and the calf of the stall."—*Christian Leader.*

"A collection of simple addresses to children, founded on the animals mentioned in Holy Writ. Teachers will find much helpful matter within its pages."—*Teachers' Aid.*

"Mr Adams writes simply and brightly in a way which children are certain to appreciate."—*S. S. Chronicle.*

EDINBURGH AND LONDON:

OLIPHANT ANDERSON & FERRIER.

And all Booksellers.

Post 8vo, cloth extra, price 1s. 6d.

Bible Stories without Names

By Rev. HARRY SMITH, M.A., Tibbermore.

"A delightful and original book for children."—*Primitive Methodist Magazine.*

"The idea of the book is as ingenious as it is simple, and it is sure to prove a source of widespread delight."—*Baptist Magazine.*

"Mr Smith has hit upon a very happy thought, and has worked out his idea with much skill."—*The Christian World.*

"The book is excellently written, beautifully printed, and artistically bound."—*Evening Times.*

"The idea of this book is novel and exceedingly well worked out. The stories are well written in language suited to children, and are thoroughly interesting."—*Church Family Newspaper.*

"The value of this book can hardly be over-estimated. Put into the hands of children for Sunday reading in the home, with some older person to guide their study and prevent discouragement in the hard places (especially if kept simply for Sunday reading), it would make the Sabbath a day to be looked forward to, and would familiarise those who used it with the location of the various Bible stories."—*Christian Advocate.*

"Altogether one of the best little text-books for inculcating a knowledge of the Scripture which we have ever seen."—*Bookseller and Stationer.*

"We like this new departure (as the author truly calls it), and predict that it will be heartily welcomed and widely used."—*Record.*

"The idea of the book is as ingenious as it is simple, and it is sure to prove a source of widespread delight."—*Baptist Magazine.*

"The stories (twenty in all) are well written in a language suited to children, and are thoroughly interesting."—*Church Family Newspaper.*

"The tales are told with quite remarkable pith and power."—*Sabbath School Magazine.*

EDINBURGH AND LONDON:

OLIPHANT, ANDERSON & FERRIER.

And all Booksellers.